THE WICKED FLEE

BY THE AUTHOR

Crime Fiction

{The Marty Singer Mysteries}

A Reason to Live

Blueblood

One Right Thing

The Spike

The Wicked Flee

{Standalone}

Stealing Sweetwater

{Short story collection}

one bad twelve

Psychological Suspense

The Kindness of Neighbors

Fantasy & Science Fiction

{Short stories}

"Sword of Kings"

"Assassin"

"Seven Into the Bleak"

"Trial By Fire" (anthologized in *Walk the Fire #2*)

THE WICKED FLEE

A Marty Singer Mystery

MATTHEW IDEN

THOMAS & MERCER

This is a work of fiction. Names, characters, organizations, places, events, and incidents are either products of the author's imagination or are used fictitiously.

Text copyright © 2014 Matthew Iden
All rights reserved.

No part of this book may be reproduced, or stored in a retrieval system, or transmitted in any form or by any means, electronic, mechanical, photocopying, recording, or otherwise, without express written permission of the publisher.

Published by Thomas & Mercer, Seattle
www.apub.com

Amazon, the Amazon logo, and Thomas & Mercer are trademarks of Amazon.com, Inc., or its affiliates.

ISBN-13: 9781477829455
ISBN-10: 1477829458

Printed in the United States of America

For Renee, who continues to make the whole thing possible.
For my family.
For my friends.

The wicked flee when no man pursueth; but the righteous are as bold as a lion.

—Proverbs 28:1

CHAPTER ONE
LAST NIGHT

Trooper First Class Sarah Haynesworth pulled her cruiser over to the side of the road and peered through the darkness and falling snow at the dented mailbox in front of her. The second number of the address was missing, but even through the flakes she could make out the stark white outline of where it had been, like a tan line from a bathing suit. On the cruiser's roof, her lights spun silently, lighting the yard in splashes of red and blue.

She pulled out the small white notebook she carried everywhere and traced her finger down the page, confirming the address from the information the girl had given her. *This is it.* But Sarah slipped the pad of paper back into a breast pocket and continued to sit, making no motion to get out of the car. Not yet. She swallowed and looked at the house, reluctant—despite her authority, her training, and the gun at her side—to leave the warmth and security of the car.

The house was like a hundred others in this part of rural Maryland. White siding gone dingy gray. A black shingle roof, swaybacked and sagging. On the side nearest her, a garage had been converted into an interior room then converted back again, although the work was all for naught, as the right-most face of the renovation slumped toward the ground, its windows broken and a section of the wall simply missing. On the far left side of the house—to call it a wing would be stretching things—feeble yellow light spilled from a window. In the front yard, a rusting blue Ford pickup sat close to the house at a haphazard angle, as if the driver hadn't felt like parking on the street and instead had driven directly to the door and hopped out. The house was silent. There was no movement other than the softly falling snow.

Sarah sighed. *That door isn't going to knock on itself, girl.* She either had to leave or investigate . . . she hadn't driven here to check out the real estate. And, if she *was* going to investigate, she needed to get her butt in gear—whoever was inside would have to be blind not to have seen her cruiser's lights.

Get out or leave.

That pretty much said it all. Moving decisively, she zipped her regulation parka up to the chin and planted her hat firmly on her head. She stepped out of the car, squinting as icy air hit her face. She reached back inside the car and turned off the reds and blues, although she left the headlights on. The light might stop after only twenty feet—it was arrested by the snow tumbling in thick, fat flakes through the beams—but it was the only outside illumination. Streetlamps were a luxury that had stopped three miles back.

The ground crunched underfoot, not only from the snow, but from the road itself, made of cinder, gravel, and ground pieces of coke residue brought in from the steel mills and coke plants just over the border in Pennsylvania. It was what many of the roads in this end of the state were made of once you got away from the highways, though she hadn't seen the ugly, reddish rocks since she was a little girl. Poor counties, left to their own devices, used whatever they could get their hands on to pave the roads.

She shut the car door and resisted the urge to lean against it, to keep steel and glass between her and the house. At five feet four and one hundred fifteen pounds, she was fully covered by the vehicle's bulk and it made her feel secure, like she was in a tank. But hiding behind her car wasn't going to give her any more answers than sitting in it.

Moving cautiously, she circled the cruiser and followed a broken slate walkway to the front of the house, sweeping her eyes left and right in continuous motion, taking in details, making assessments. Despite the winter temperatures, the screen door was still in place, the material ripped and hanging away like a dog's ear. For safety's sake, she took a half step to the right of the doorway to get herself out of the most common line of fire as she reached the door. She pushed a small doorbell, then rapped firmly on the metal frame of the screen. The sound was shockingly loud in the stillness of the winter night. She tipped her head, listening carefully for noises or movement. Her hand squeezed and resqueezed the butt of her pistol. If she wasn't careful, she'd get a cramp in her hand and she made a conscious effort to relax her arm and shoulder. She'd taken her gloves off when she'd climbed out of the car, and the butt of the gun was cold in her hand.

When there was no answer, she knocked again using the fat of her fist and shouted, "Maryland State Police!"

She cocked her head. A muffled thump had made its way to her from inside. A chair tipping over and caught a second too late? She unsnapped the holster's safety strap on her sidearm.

A distant bang now, farther away than the thump. Not like a gun or a backfire. Like . . . like an old-fashioned screen door, the kind that didn't have the piston to keep it from slamming shut after it had been opened too far. The ones they used to put on the back door leading from the kitchen to the yard.

She took off running around the side of the house, pulling both her Maglite and her gun as she went. The flashlight lit the night in a twenty-foot circle and she played it left to right, trying to cover as large an area as she could while sprinting for the back of the house. Her breath plumed in the night air.

Sarah rounded the corner at a jog. Fifty feet away, a pale form was hunched over a pile of something, dragging it to the back of the property. A wide trench in the snow led in a straight line from the house's back door to the deep mountain woods that edged the yard.

"State police," she hollered, training both her flashlight and her gun on the form. "Hold it!"

Without a sound, the figure dropped what it was doing and ran straight into the woods. An arrest, not a fatality, was the goal, so Sarah took up the chase, cursing at the gear on her belt that jangled and swung as she moved. She tried keeping the man pinned in the beam of the Maglite, but her own movement jerked her aim back and forth off her target. The man was a stark white blur and she realized with a start that he was shirtless. And a quick glance at the footprints in front of her told her a shirt wasn't the only all-weather gear he was missing—he wasn't wearing any shoes.

She stopped when she reached the thing the man had been dragging. The pile had arms and legs, long blonde hair, a glassy stare. Sarah knelt, checking the neck and wrist. Cold, no pulse. Gone. She got to her feet and sprinted after the form, slipping in the foot-high drifts. The blur dashed into the woods and out of view. Sarah reached the tree line a second later, ducking her head under a low-hanging pine bough loaded with snow. Tears streamed from her eyes from the cold and she had to continually wipe her running nose as she peered at the ground. Deer trails—some faint, some pounded flat—snaked away in all directions, but the man's tracks pointed the way dead ahead.

She flicked the flashlight back and forth, searching for the ghost-white form, but the Maglite's beam splashed against the trees closest to her, ruining her night vision. Playing it along the ground instead, she followed the barefoot trail, alternating the cone of light from a middle distance to directly in front of her every few seconds. Underfoot, the forest floor swelled and dipped from the gnarled pine roots hiding beneath the drifts, and she had to fight to keep her balance as the hillside dipped into a gully.

The tracks chased the line of the hillside down. Snow was thinner here in the thick of the woods, lying in patches on the ground rather than blankets thanks to the shelter of the trees, but slick Piedmont granite and inch-thick ice made running even more hazardous. She scrambled down the trail awkwardly, using one hand to aim the Maglite, the other to keep her service pistol at the ready. At several points, though, the pitch was too steep, and she had to use her gun hand to hold on to saplings and branches for support, violating every commandment she'd ever been taught in books or classes.

Slow down, girl. This is a marathon, now, not a sprint. Time was on her side. Barefoot and shirtless? In January? This guy wasn't going to make it ten more minutes. She slowed and placed her feet self-consciously. All she had to do was stay alert, keep herself safe, and follow the tracks.

But halfway down the slope, the beam showed her the prints simply . . . vanished.

She whipped the flashlight from left to right, but the ground revealed only virgin snow. She pointed the beam overhead, above where the tracks disappeared, but saw only thin, horizontal pine branches going across the deer trail, too fragile to support a climber. She slowed, shuffling in a circle to pan the area to the left and right of the path—then cried out as her ankle caught on a raised tree root, snagged as firmly as a noose.

Her feet went out from under her and she landed belly-first on a slab of granite, with her head pointing down the slope. Both the Maglite and her gun flew from her hand like she'd thrown them. She could only watch as the gun hit a patch of bare rock and skittered away while her flashlight tumbled to the bottom of the gully, the beam spinning crazily in the darkness as it fell.

Moving painfully, Sarah struggled to her hands and knees. The skin of her palms was on fire from where she'd scraped them on the ice. The impact knocked the wind from her and she gulped and hiccupped, trying to keep calm as her body convulsed in the effort to breathe. It was hard to remember that having the wind knocked out of you was medically harmless when it felt as if you were being suffocated. With an effort, she rose to one knee, her eyes pinned on the Maglite below, and was getting ready to make the push to get to her feet when a dark form passed in front of the beam.

Then the light went out.

Sarah froze. Adrenaline shot through her system and she fought to keep the panic down, but without the flashlight, the night instantly closed in around her, cold and vicious. No moon lit the sky. Stars were hidden by the pine boughs overhead. Complete blindness was held at bay only by the high contrast of the snowbanks against the darker tree boles, but the shapes were indistinct and threatening, as likely to be a man as a tree.

Everything she had went into the act of listening. To reduce the noise, she breathed through her mouth. Her pulse sounded heavy and loud in her ears. She was painfully aware that her blue uniform was a dark blob against the snow and that the rough synthetic material sounded like two pieces of sandpaper rubbing together when she moved. The night was deadly quiet . . . then her head snapped around at the sound of a dull thump on her left. Just a raft of snow, too heavy for a bough, falling to the ground.

She moved to a large tree on her right, trying to melt into the darkness of its bulky shadow. Slowly, she lifted the wide-brimmed campaign hat off her head and set it on the ground beside her. It hindered her vision at the best of times and right now it was making her positively claustrophobic. Ice crystals she hadn't felt before tickled her cheeks and ears and a wider range of sounds came to her. A barred owl hooted in the distance, and there was a light ticking noise nearby—a frozen branch rubbing against a neighbor, maybe, or a single beech leaf fluttering in the wind. Otherwise, the night had the crystal depths of deep winter, marred only by the crunching of the snow.

Crunching?

Sarah spun in place at the sound of footsteps to her right, then a figure sprang at her. She saw the silhouette of a raised arm and threw her own up instinctively to block the blow, but it was desperate and late and most of the force from her own Maglite slammed into her shoulder. The blow landed on the meaty part of her upper arm and not bone, but she yelled out at the pain. The man came at her, breathing in ragged gasps as he swung the flashlight in wide, wild arcs. She ducked and dodged blindly, guessing as much as sensing where to go to keep from having her head caved in. He raised the flashlight overhead for a colossal swing and she backed away desperately, only to trip over another tree root.

The swing was close enough that she felt the air move as it passed her face; then she was tumbling backward, landing painfully on her back. The man's complete miss threw him off balance too, however, and his momentum carried him forward to trip over the same root that had dumped Sarah. He landed with a gasp next to her, near enough that she could feel his breath on her neck. Rather than get to her feet, she reached out to grab a wrist or an elbow, but the instant he felt her touch, he hollered and threw a wild punch.

Their struggle became a wrestling match in the snow, a grunting tangle of twigs, arms, and dirt. Academy training had given her a good ground game—something she'd needed since she was routinely a foot shorter than everyone else—but the man had hung on to the Maglite and rained blows on her back and neck. With no shirt, he was harder to grab than any opponent she'd had to collar on the mat before and as she clutched at him, a lucky kick caught her in the stomach, stunning her. The man scrambled away, trying to get the necessary distance to swing the flashlight for a knockout blow.

Desperately, Sarah clawed at her belt with her good hand. The man shouted and whipped the flashlight over his head once more. But she ripped the stun gun from its holster, lunged forward, and stabbed it into the man's ribs. His shriek drowned out the sound of the flat, electric zap. A second later he was down on the ground, writhing and flopping like a fish on a hook.

She stayed on her hands and knees for a minute, her chest heaving as she caught her breath. Her belly and back ached and her hands burned with scrapes where they weren't numb from the crushing cold. She kept an eye on the man as she sucked in great lungfuls of air, trying to recover. The stun gun was in one hand, and she was ready to apply the business end to the man's body all night long if she had to.

After a long minute, she felt good enough to stand. She wiped her nose on the back of her hand and looked down at her prize. The man was flapping his arms like a bat in slow motion, desperate to run but unable to make the motion translate into effective movement.

Relying on her sense of touch in the darkness, Sarah patted down the parts of him that were actually clothed, then flipped him over in the snow and cuffed him. Leaving him facedown where he was, she began a crawling search for the Maglite. Blind, she moved in small arcs away from the spot of their fight, sweeping her arms back and forth until eventually she found it under an inkberry bush. She flipped it on with a sigh. It felt like the first break she'd gotten all night. With the help of the flashlight she found her gun under a rock shelf and breathed a second sigh of relief—more of the administrative sort, this time. Lose your sidearm, no matter what the reason, and you could expect an ass-chewing to remember from Lieutenant Kline.

"H-h-hey," the man said, finally recovered enough to speak. "I'm-m-m *freezing* to d-d-death over here."

She ignored him, busy looking for her hat, which she found at the base of the tree where she'd left it. When she had it safely on her head, with the brim squared just so, she walked over to the man and pulled him to his feet. Despite an odd, jutting potbelly, overall he was a scrawny thirtysomething, with his ribs showing prominently through the pink, nearly frozen skin of his chest. As she thought, he was shoeless and shirtless and if she hadn't caught him, he would've been lucky to make it through the next hour alive.

"Are you Kevin Handley?"

"G-g-go f-f-fuck yourself," he said. "Nig-g-ger."

She hooked a foot around one ankle, pushed him in the opposite direction, and pitched him face-first into the nearest snowbank. Her boot kept him in that position as he squirmed and shouted muffled obscenities into the snow. She counted off twenty seconds, then grabbed his hair and pulled his head back.

"No one's going to know the difference between you running naked into the woods in the middle of the night in January and me holding you down in a snowbank for the next half hour," she said. "You want to lose your nose to frostbite, it's okay by me."

He stuttered another curse and she pushed him back into the snow. She counted to twenty-two this time and pulled him out. "Kevin Handley, yes or no?"

"Y-y-y-yes," he gasped.

"Is that Tiffany Chilton in your yard?"

His mouth worked in a funny way and Sarah moved to push him back down. "Yes! Y-y-yes. Tiffany something. That's all I know."

Sarah smiled for the first time that night. "Thank you for your cooperation, Mr. Handley. Now let's get you somewhere warm and secure. I think I know a place."

CHAPTER TWO

The goddess of sleep had folded her angel wings around me. The sandman had tossed a bag of magic dust in my eyes. Consciousness was a distant, somewhat unpleasant, memory. And all it had taken to achieve this state was a low-grade fever, a ninety-minute coughing jag, and a half bottle of NyQuil.

I was in the second week of an illness so severe that to call it a cold seemed laughable—but laughing brought on a new round of coughing, so I'd been avoiding any form of comedy for a while. I hated winter colds. They were my least favorite way of being sick. Scratch that, *second* least favorite way. Cancer took the cake, of course, and I'd had my fill of that particular bug. But colds came in a close second. They made me feel so . . . *bleh*. Not quite sick enough to see the doctor, too miserable to do anything except sit and read or watch TV. Sleep had been elusive and the gray January winter coupled with my cold made everything colorless and bleak, such that I found myself wishing for sticky Virginia summers just for something new to complain about.

With enough self-medication and plain old exhaustion, however, my body had finally thrown in the towel and, for the first night in a week, I'd floated away on dreamy green clouds, something I hadn't managed much of since picking up the bug around New Year's Eve. Like most drug- and sickness-induced sleeps, though, it wasn't a sound slumber. Hazy dreams—of steam baths and Mentho-Lyptus cocktails and a lab-coated octopus wrapping tentacles around my chest—mixed with reality, and I had the strangest feeling that the octopus had taken one tentacle and knocked on my chest instead of squeezing it to a pulp.

My eyes snapped open. The knocking wasn't part of the dream—it was part of the reality. Someone was pounding on my front door. Aggressively. I groaned, threw back the cover, and swung my feet over the side of the bed. Pierre, my cat, jumped to the floor with a thud from his position near my feet and ran into the hall, assuming that if the human was standing, it was time to eat.

I glanced at the nightstand clock. *9:17 p.m.* The sweatpants I'd been living in for the past ten days were within easy reach, so I slipped them on, threw a fleece over my head, and pulled my SIG Sauer from the nightstand drawer. Thirty years on Washington, DC's Homicide squad had given me habits that were hard to break.

The pounding continued during the time it took me to reach the landing, jog down the stairs, and cross the living room. I glanced through the peephole, then unlocked the door. On the other side was a young, whip-thin Asian man sporting perfectly spiked hair, a puffy winter coat made out of some metallic material, and wraparound shades despite the pitch-black night. A piercing through one eyebrow and five rings through his right ear made him look like the average punk at a rave, but I knew it was all part of the persona for Chuck Rhee, an Arlington PD detective specializing in the gangs that roamed Northern Virginia along the DC border, and a friend of mine.

"Chuck?" I said, my voice phlegmy. "What the hell are you doing here?"

"Marty," Rhee said, his voice tight, the syllables clipped. "I need your help."

"Come on in," I said, taking a step back. I shut the door and turned on some lights. "Coffee?"

Rhee shook his head. He wouldn't sit, instead standing with his hands jammed into the pockets of his coat. Tense, angry. A coil of wire, ready to snap or spring. "Can't. I got a problem."

"You take on gangbangers eight hours a day. What's bad enough that you're calling it a problem?"

"It's Lucy. My sister. She's gone."

My cough medicine buzz melted away. "Talk to me."

"We were supposed to have dinner around five," Rhee said, running a hand through his hair. "I got off my shift at four. I told her I'd pick her up at our grandparents' place."

"That's where she lives?"

"Yeah. I'm gone too often to look after her and my grandparents live near a decent high school, so she's with them. I give them some cash to help with bills," he said. "Anyway, she's not there and my grandparents told me they hadn't seen her since she left this morning. I called her phone a million times and no answer."

"Okay."

Rhee paced to the couch and back. "I know. Teenager misses a dinner date with her older brother. That's not weird, it's normal. And maybe her phone's off or not charged or she don't feel like answering."

"You wouldn't be this upset if it was typical teenage crap."

Rhee let out a breath. "Lucy don't miss things like this. She don't forget to call. She don't blow off family. Not since our parents died. She ain't no saint; she just does what she says she's gonna do. If she don't want to do something, she says so. If she's going to be late, she calls."

"Okay," I said. I sank into a chair. "What are you thinking?"

He shook his head. "I don't know. I filed a report, but no evidence of foul play, you know? At sixteen, she's just a runaway to half the departments around."

"They'll listen to a cop, though."

"Yeah, and my buddies in Arlington are following up right now, but . . ." He trailed off.

"Not good enough."

"No," Rhee said and raised his head to look at me. "Singer, I've seen kids on the street, the ones the gangs recruit. Or sell. Four hours is a lifetime. They can be across the state line in an hour. They can be in another time zone in eight. I can't wait for this to make its way through the system. I need to tackle this myself. Now."

I nodded. "Where do we start?"

CHAPTER THREE

Eddie Molter prowled the streets of Woodbridge, trying to find the dump that matched the address he'd been given.

He hated this part of Virginia. He didn't know it like he knew Maryland or the stretch between DC and Baltimore. The town was smashed up against the highway on one side and Route 1 on the other, with enough strip malls and check-cashing stores and Pollo Locos vomiting cars onto the roads to make driving seem a lot like taking part in a demolition derby, even late on a Saturday night.

It didn't help that he had no idea where the hell he was going while making the most important drive of his life. The map on his phone was nice, but Eddie liked to drive, not navigate, and he was terrible at it. All Gerry had given him was an address, a few landmarks, and one telltale sign to follow: when he spotted the biggest black-and-silver Raiders banner he'd ever seen in his life, he'd found the right place.

"His name's Tuck?" he'd asked Gerry when he first got the call. "How do you know him?"

"He worked a construction job up here, near Columbia. He came in for a girl every night. When he wasn't busting heads over at the Roadhouse, I mean."

"How'd he get in touch with you?"

"When you told me you were looking for something . . . special, I passed it on," Gerry had said, unsure if he was in trouble with Eddie or not. "He'd already asked me if we had some work, so I didn't think it would hurt to pull him in."

"Did you give him my name?"

"No! No way," Gerry said, quick to reassure his boss. "I just told him you'd call and that he'd better not be bullshitting."

And that's how Eddie came to be lost in the back end of Woodbridge. The map said he was less than a mile from his destination, but he felt like he could be across the street from the place and he wouldn't know where he was. Time to call.

He dialed the number with a thumb, and waited. Two rings, then a voice answered, low and lazy. "Yeah?"

"Is this Tuck?"

"Yeah." The grunt barely made it through the crash and bang of TV commercials in the background. "Who's this?"

"Gerry's friend," Eddie said. "I'm about ten minutes away. Do you have what I came for?"

"Ready and waiting," Tuck said.

"I'm looking for a Raiders banner? Anything else?"

A pause. "I'll be on the porch."

"See you in ten," Eddie said and hung up, wondering what kind of idiot he was dealing with. It was pitch black out and below freezing. All the dude had to do was flick a porch light on and off to let Eddie know where to pull over, but he wanted to stand sentry. Whatever. At least Eddie didn't need to know what Tuck looked like now—he was going to be the only numb-nuts standing outside on his deck.

He took a left off of Route 1 onto Featherstone Road and cruised past the duplex homes and garden apartments. Frost had built up on the side of the road and fogged the windows of parked cars and apartments alike. A quick glance at the map, another left, and a minute later he spotted the Raiders banner rising and falling in the breeze.

Standing on the porch to one side of the banner and backlit by an open door was a stocky figure in jeans and a T-shirt. Tuck, evidently. His hands were jammed into his pockets, the only concession to the cold. Eddie stopped the car at the bottom of the porch steps and got out.

Taking in the flat stare and the crooked nose—busted multiple times—the set of the shoulders and planted feet, Eddie sighed to himself and tried to keep his face as expressionless as possible. The guy was an open book, just another knucklehead who liked to swing first and talk later. Bar brawls and parking lot fights were probably weekly events. It didn't matter. He didn't need to have an in-depth discussion with the guy. He needed to grab what he came for, pay the man, and leave.

"Tuck?" Eddie asked, coming up the steps. He got a grunt in reply, then the guy—a kid, really, but built like a brick shithouse—turned and opened the screen door to go inside. Eddie followed him.

The entrance spilled directly into the living room. It was about what Eddie had expected to find. A TV that probably cost more than Tuck's car—but propped up by cinder blocks and a sheet of plywood—dominated the room. Gaming consoles and a stereo were connected to it, the connecting wires spilling onto the floor haphazardly. Tower speakers flanked the jury-rigged entertainment center. Cans of low-end beer and forty-ounce malt liquor bottles lay scattered around the room. A few posters of heavyweight MMA fighters had been tacked or taped to the walls. Smells of food and mold lingered in the room despite the blast of cold air they'd brought with them.

Sitting in a broken recliner in the far corner was a ginger-haired, fish-eyed dude with a wispy mustache. He ogled Eddie like he'd seen an alien. On one end of a beat-up, rust-colored couch—the only other piece of furniture in the room—was a long-legged blond guy cultivating a stoner look with a plaid shirt, black watch cap, and a half-baked goatee. He looked back at Eddie and blinked a few times, as though he had expected one thing to walk through the door and found to his surprise that something very different had shown up.

Tuck gestured to the first one, then the other. "Ookie. Che. They're cool."

Slacker housemates. Eddie dismissed them and looked at Tuck. "Where?"

"This way," Tuck said, then motioned to Che. "You're gonna want to see this."

"What are you doing?" Eddie asked, irritated. "This ain't a joke."

"They're going to know, anyway," Tuck said, pushing back. "If I said they're cool, they're cool."

Eddie shrugged and put a bored look on his face. "It's on you if they talk about it."

Tuck looked like he wanted to get in his grill for that, but he turned around and led the three of them down a corridor to the bedrooms. Ookie, not invited, came down the hall anyway, trailing the others. Tuck's bedroom was closed and he took out a set of keys and unlocked it, then opened the door and threw the light on.

On the bed was a slim Asian girl with glossy black hair down to the middle of her back. She wore jeans and a pink warm-up jacket. She lay sprawled on the bed like she'd been tossed from the doorway and was either asleep or unconscious.

"Is that . . . ?" Che asked, surprise in his voice.

"Yeah," Tuck said, smirking. "I brought her in while you losers were at work."

"She got a story?" Eddie asked. He sat on the edge of the bed and gently grasped the girl's chin, tilting her head back and forth, looking for bruises or cuts, then gingerly peeled back her lips to look at her teeth. The girl moaned softly as Eddie moved her.

"We used to hang," Tuck said, crossing his arms and leaning against the door frame. "She wouldn't put out. Took a swing at me when I tried to get some."

"Yeah?" Eddie said, not bothering to look at Tuck. In the same gentle manner he'd used to manipulate her head, he rolled her jeans up to check her calves, then did the same with the sleeves of the jacket and peered at her forearms and wrists. He silently approved. No tracks, no bruises, no rashes, no signs of self-abuse. "Did she connect?"

Tuck grunted but said nothing. Eddie heard the one friend, Che, shuffle from foot to foot.

"What did you use on her?"

"Roofies," Tuck said.

"She do drugs? Booze?"

"No drugs," Tuck said. "Drank some, not much."

"Did you ever sleep with her?"

"Nope."

Eddie shot him a look.

"Believe me, man, I would remember," Tuck said.

"She screw anyone else?"

"If she didn't want some of this, she didn't want it from nobody."

Eddie smiled. "Yeah, okay. What about your two buddies? They fool around while she was knocked out?"

"Man, they didn't even know she was here."

Eddie looked at Che full-on. "Is that right?"

"Didn't know, man," Che said.

Eddie held the stare for a second, then turned it on Ookie, but snorted and turned back at the girl on the bed. "She got a family?"

"Older brother. He's never around," Tuck said. "No parents."

"She's got to sleep somewhere."

"She lives with her grandparents."

"Are they going to be a problem?"

Tuck shook his head. "They don't know English, don't have cell phones. She does everything for them. Buys their food, pays the bills. They're clueless."

Eddie stood, nodded. "Does she have a purse? A wallet? Phone?"

"Yeah," Tuck said reluctantly.

"Get them," Eddie said. "If somebody calls or wants to see her ID, I'm not going to sit there with my thumb up my ass."

Tuck disappeared for a minute, came back carrying a leather purse. He handed it over and Eddie rifled through it, making sure the essentials were there. He pulled out a smartphone with a Hello Kitty cover on it.

He held it up, looking at Tuck. "Locked?"

Tuck shrugged. "I never knew the code."

Eddie snapped the purse shut and slung it over a shoulder. "Does she have a coat?"

"She had one. I don't know where it is."

"Well, grab something, asshole," Eddie said. "I'm not going to let her freeze to death."

Tuck's eyes narrowed and his jaw and fists bunched. Eddie hadn't moved from the edge of the bed, but he shifted slightly to square his shoulders to the punk. Behind Tuck, both friends swayed a little in place, but didn't move. The look on their faces was noncommittal.

"I don't have time to screw around," Eddie said, staring back at Tuck. "Do you want your money or not?"

Tuck took a deep breath and told Ookie to get the fuck out of the way so he could look in the closet. He dug around for a minute, then pulled out an old hoodie. Eddie tilted the girl upright and the two of them dressed her clumsily. When they were finished, he reached into an inner pocket and pulled out a wad of bills. He quickly counted off a dozen twenties, folded them in half, and handed them to Tuck.

He turned back to the girl, carefully arranging her head and hair on the pillow as if she were a model posing for a photo shoot. Which turned out to be partially right—he pulled out a phone and took several pictures, careful to capture her face and hair. Then, with no effort, Eddie swung the girl over one shoulder, and everyone stomped out of the bedroom to the front of the house. Tuck walked onto the porch and glanced around the neighborhood. But it was after eleven on a frozen Saturday night. People weren't looking out windows or standing in yards; they were huddled on the couch or in bed. Tuck signaled to Eddie and held the door for him as he carried the girl outside.

Eddie turned to look at Tuck before he was off the porch. "Hey, what's her name?"

"Lucy," Tuck said. "Lucy Rhee."

CHAPTER FOUR

We were standing inside the foyer of Ultra, a nightclub east of Washington Circle. From the outside, it resembled any other office building in downtown DC with its faux marble columns, darkened double glass doors, planters to either side of the lintel. But the line of fifty at the door—huddling their bodies together for warmth in scant miniskirts and ripped jeans, their breath not so much steaming as crystallizing in the air around them—proclaimed Ultra was the place to *be* in the city. Tonight, at least.

A flash of Chuck's badge had gotten us past the bouncers, sparking grumbles and complaints the length of the line. One doorman glared at the hopeful partiers, quieting them down, while the other opened the door, releasing a blast of noise, heat, and humidity. Chuck and I squeezed past the muscle and into the club, blinking and squinting to adjust. Inside, the clientele was hip, young, and diverse. What it wasn't was old, white, and tired, which meant Chuck fit right in and I looked like I'd driven in from the burbs to pick up my kids.

"I think you should do the talking," I yelled into Chuck's ear.

"Yeah, that's probably a good idea," Chuck shouted back, grinning. Then the grin slid off his face as he remembered why we were here. He jerked his head toward the dance floor. "Drinks are upstairs. I know the bartender."

We pushed and slid our way through the press of flesh, tapping shoulders and guiding sweaty bodies out of the way. The thud and crash of techno dance music was too loud to ask politely. Or rudely, for that matter. Dry ice—that old club favorite—wafted up from vents in the floor and I wondered what Hieronymus Bosch might've thought of the place. Guttural bass notes pounded from eight-foot speakers, making me wince at the echo it made in my stuffy head, not to mention the way it plucked at something in my gut south of my stomach. It wasn't the only hazard, either. More than once, we had to duck as several dancers—zonked out on pills, powders, or sprays—whipped neon glow sticks around like propellers.

Chuck led the way to an industrial-looking spiral staircase of steel and glass that twisted its way to a second-floor catwalk. Dancers, more subdued than their comrades on the first floor, lined the railing, taking a break to grab a drink and watch the seething mass below. Most were teens and twentysomethings, though a few of the voyeurs were men in the throes of midlife crises, doing their best to look half their age. But the clothes and the hair—but most of all, the discomfort on their faces—gave them away. I grimaced. I knew which category I was in.

I trailed Chuck to a bar set back from the catwalk, a block of smoked glass with a dramatic streak of white marble shot through, like a comet going through a night sky. Chuck sauntered up to it and waited until he caught the eye of a young Latina girl behind it. She brightened and came over and he leaned over the bar so they could kiss cheeks. A sparkling name tag on her bosom said "MIXOLOGIST." She glanced at me, then she looked back at Chuck, tilting her head so she could hear him.

"I'm looking for Lucy," he yelled. "You seen her around?"

She shook her head. "Not tonight. Her posse's here, though."

"Who?"

"Leila and Cupie. In the lounge. Alfredo let them in."

"Oh, yeah?" Chuck said. Even through the thundering music, I could hear the not-quite-pleased tone, but he gave her hand a squeeze. "Thanks."

"What's the lounge?" I asked as Chuck led the way back to the catwalk.

"Special treatment," he yelled over a shoulder. "Champagne, dope, celebrities. Invitation only."

"And Alfredo?"

"The owner. He likes to play it big. Says he's from Buenos Aires or Rio or something, but he probably grew up in Virginia Beach. He invites the girls he spots on the dance floor, especially the underage ones."

"Sounds like quality material."

Chuck made a face and nodded. I took out a tissue and blew my nose as we walked to the opposite side from the bar, passing the catwalk we'd climbed. We stopped at a small landing with a frosted-glass door. "*V.I.P.*" was etched into it in an ultracool sans serif font. I'd have to watch it or my self-esteem was going to take a nosedive. Even the doors here were more hip than I was.

Another walking muscle stood to the left of the entrance to the lounge. He was dressed in the standard, clichéd dance club security wear: black suit, wraparound shades, close-cropped black hair. He was also big enough to have bounced the bouncers at the front door.

"Polo," Chuck said, nodding to the guard. They bumped fists. Chuck's looked like a baby rattle next to the other. "You mind asking Alfredo if he can spare a minute?"

"Important?"

"Very."

"Hold on." The bouncer opened the frosted door and disappeared. I waited until the door closed behind him. "Polo?"

Chuck glanced over. "His real name's Ralph. People weren't taking him seriously, so he told everybody to start calling him Polo—like Ralph Lauren, you know?—or he'd twist their head off and put it in a can."

I gave a short nod. "Polo it is."

The door opened a minute later and Polo leaned out, holding the door and motioning for us to come in. Chuck and I sauntered through and looked around.

It was what I'd expected. Leather couches, a wet bar, low lighting. The far wall was floor-to-ceiling one-way glass so the VIP set could watch the plebes having their fun far below, but the room was nearly soundproofed, so the scene felt oddly disjointed. Only the thud of the bass shaking the glass hinted at the decibel level just a few feet away.

Couches and easy chairs were arranged in intimate groupings of three and four. Most were occupied by curvy, model-worthy women and well-dressed young men laughing too loudly. I spotted more than one local sports celebrity with champagne in one hand and a girl in the other, looking uncomfortable in suits instead of uniforms—the collars too tight, the material straining over chests and thighs. Polo pointed to the back of the lounge and we wound our way through the low glass tables and cushy furniture to a corner of the room. Along the way, Chuck glanced to his left, then did an almost imperceptible double take. He covered it well and we kept moving until we found our target.

Open bottles of Cristal and Cîroc littered a long table already crowded with champagne flutes and lowball glasses. Someone's drink had spilled and the liquid had formed a clear, kidney-shaped puddle on the glass that shivered in time to the music.

On the couch behind the table reclined a man in his thirties. Tan or dark complexion, clean shaven. Short black hair on his head, a jungle of it on the chest. He wore a white shirt with three buttons open at the top. It seemed a weird throwback to some darker age of fashion, like 1973, which I could've told him from personal experience had been more of an accident than a plan. Long arms were spread along the back of the couch, caressing the shoulders of the girls on either side of him. A large white guy, as big as Polo, sprawled at the other end of the couch with a girl half his size on his knee. She looked like a ventriloquist's doll. The two were in their own little world, giggling at something. Two young girls, looking waifish and annoyed, sat in a leather chair to one side, one in the seat, the other on the arm. They stiffened when they saw Chuck.

"Detective," Alfredo said, expansively. "What a pleasure."

"Alfredo," Chuck said, nodding.

The club owner looked at me, raised an eyebrow. "Who's the underdressed dude with you checking me out like I'm a piece of meat?"

"This is a friend of mine, Marty Singer."

"He ever hear of a dress code?"

"He don't clean up too good," Chuck said. "He wanted to wear sweatpants."

Alfredo sniffed a small laugh. "What can I do for you?"

"I need to talk to these two," Chuck said, jerking his head toward the girls on the chair.

"That it? I thought you were after something serious," Alfredo laughed.

"Nope. Just a talk. Then we're out of your hair."

"Well, that sounds easy," Alfredo said, then his face changed to something coy and he quirked an eyebrow. "Unless you two are looking for something young and exciting?"

"No time, man," Chuck said. I could almost see his teeth grinding together. It was hard to play patty-cake with some asshole when the clock was ticking.

"That's not the normal—what do you call it?—MO for Detective Rhee."

"It is tonight," Chuck said. "Just the way it has to be."

Alfredo shrugged, then Don Juan's attention turned to me. "That's too bad. What do you say, old man? You on the prowl for some underage pussy?"

"Thank you, no," I said. "I'm having enough trouble with the middle-aged kind."

"Nothing a couple of Viagra won't cure, my friend. Or, in your case, maybe the whole bottle," he said, getting a laugh out of the entourage. "You ain't looking so hot, you don't mind me saying."

"My problems are more about commitment and sharing. You know, old people stuff."

"If you say so, man. You sure that's the only thing going on?"

"Well, maybe if you'd let us talk to these two girls so we could get what we came for, I could get back to working on my flagging relationship."

"Did you say *flagging*?" he asked, putting a hand to his ear. "Or *fagging*? I mean, I don't want to tell you how to live your life, homie, but I think I know what your problem is."

The sycophants tittered. I looked at him, tired. I'd tried. "Will you please stop being an asshole? You're not that funny and we don't have the time for you to learn."

As comebacks go, it wasn't much, but Alfredo had wanted to play and didn't appreciate my businesslike attitude. His heretofore friendly face darkened and he turned toward some kind of intercom thing over his shoulder, probably to summon Polo and have us thrown out on our keisters. Our night would've no doubt progressed along familiar lines from that point, but we didn't have the time to let it unfold normally . . . and I wasn't the only one who wasn't in the mood to play games.

Chuck took a step to Alfredo's side and, in one smooth motion, pulled his gun and placed his hand—firearm and all—on the man's shoulder. Not pointing it at him, not threatening him with it. Just kind of leaving it there. Like a human gun rest. Despite the fact that only a few people could've seen Chuck move, it seemed as though everyone in the room knew instantly that something was very wrong. Chatter stopped like a switch had been thrown and suddenly even the sound of a small cough was noticeable. A girl behind us whispered, "Oh my God." I was quite cognizant of the fact that there were some large, possibly heavily armed, people between us and the exit.

"Alfredo. Alfie. Al. I don't have time for your bullshit," Chuck said in a conversational tone. "I need to talk to these girls and I need to talk to them now."

Keeping his body still, Alfredo said carefully, "It's like that, huh?"

"Yes," Chuck said. "It is exactly like that."

Alfredo paused. The room held its collective breath. "All right, gentlemen. Be my guest. You want a private place to talk?"

"That would be nice," Chuck said, slipping his gun back in his holster. The room relaxed.

The club owner punched a small button behind the couch and Polo appeared. Alfredo gestured. "Show these two to the office. Give them ten minutes."

Chuck gestured to the two girls on the chair. One shot him a stubborn look and he said impatiently, "Cupie, come on. I'm not here to ruin your night. I just need to talk to you for a sec and then you can do whatever you want."

"God," she said, huffing, but got to her feet. The other one—Leila I deduced—followed her lead and the four of us turned to go. Alfredo tried one parting shot.

"I'm disappointed, Detective," he called.

Chuck turned. "Yeah?"

"I'm not a fan of being threatened in my own establishment. Don't expect any more drinks on the house."

"You keep company with shits like Bobby Carrillo, you won't have any drinks to serve. *Comprende, amigo?*" When Alfredo didn't say anything he followed it with, "That means *Understand, asshole?*"

"I know what it means," he said.

"Who's Bobby Carrillo?" I asked. "He a hockey player or something?"

Chuck, never taking his eyes off Alfredo, said, "No, man. The guy living large there in the lounge. He's MLA's top dog ever since Felix Rodriguez took a bullet in the face."

"Nice," I said. "I'm surprised no one's raided the place on a busy Saturday night and hauled everyone in for questioning."

"Yeah," Chuck said. "Surprising."

"You got what you want," Alfredo said, waving us away. "Get the fuck out of here."

We trooped out of the quiet corner and into the main body of the lounge. Polo led us around a fluid, curvy bend in the wall that I hadn't noticed coming in. Another frosted-glass door that I was betting wasn't simple glass stood in our way. There was a keypad next to it and a camera hovering blatantly above. Shielding the view with his body, Polo punched a number into the pad, opened the door, and showed us into a small but functional office with three desks and wide computer screens, all dark. The four of us squeaked past Polo and into the office as he held the door.

"Boss said ten minutes, Chuck," Polo said.

"We'll be out of here in five," Chuck said.

The bouncer nodded and left, shutting the door behind him.

"They trust you in here?" I asked when we were alone.

"They're dumb but they ain't stupid," Chuck said, pointing his chin toward the ceiling. A tiny red light glowed in the darkened corner, showing where one camera, at least, was trained on us. "Anyway, Alfredo knows I'm Arlington PD."

"No jurisdiction."

"Yeah. I mean, he knows it wouldn't take much to get some cooperation from your old squad and make life suck for him. But as long as I don't push too hard and he don't ask for too much, then we can get along."

"Using his shoulder as a gun rack is pushing pretty hard," I said.

"Yeah," he said. "I'm a little on edge."

Cupie sighed, loudly and dramatically. Chuck turned to her. "You in some kind of hurry?"

"We just got invited to the lounge tonight. I don't want to talk to a *cop* when I could be hanging with 'Fredo."

"A *cop*, huh?" Chuck said. "What happened to *Lucy's big brother*? The one whose car you puked in this summer? The one who drove you home at three in the morning and didn't tell your mom?"

The girls didn't say anything. Leila, a thin blonde with black mascara that had been artfully applied to make it look like she'd been crying, sat down on the edge of one of the desks, hugging her arms to herself.

Chuck made a noise of disgust. "Look, I don't care—too much—what you're doing here. You gotta make your own choices, even if some of them are dumb. Party all night, you want to. Drink like a fish, smoke shit in the bathroom, whatever. But use your head, especially around Alfredo. He tells you to sleep with someone or go home with some gangbanger, call me, okay?"

They were quiet. Cupie, mouth pinched, looked at one of the computer screens like there was something interesting there. Leila continued to hug herself. I glanced at Chuck and raised my eyebrows. Chuck nodded, looking tired.

"All right, that was my after-school special. All I wanted to ask is if you know where Lucy is. She supposed to go out with you tonight?"

Cupie, still miffed, said nothing, but Leila shook her head.

"That a no?" Chuck asked sharply.

"No," Leila said. "She told us she was going to have dinner with you."

"Then what?"

"She said she was going to go bowling."

"Bowling?" Chuck asked, nonplussed. "She goes bowling?"

"It's a joke," Cupie said, exasperated. "She said that when she was going to see Tuck. He's got a head like a bowling ball."

Chuck swore. "That loser? I thought she'd dropped him."

"She did. But he kept calling and calling and calling. Said all he wanted was to talk. She caved and told him she'd meet."

"Where?"

Both girls shrugged. Chuck asked, "Where'd they usually go? They have a favorite place?"

They shrugged again. Standing next to him, I could feel Chuck's frustration begin to mount and stepped in. "Is Tuck this guy's real name?"

Cupie rolled her eyes. "God, can we go?"

"*Is Tuck his real name?*" Chuck asked, an edge to his voice that made both girls flinch.

There was a second of silence, then, in a small voice, Cupie said, "I don't know. Everyone calls him Tuck."

"You know where he lives?" I asked.

"Woodbridge, I think. Off Route 1, by the Walmart. I've never been there, but Lucy went once or twice."

"You have an address? A building number? Anything?"

Leila shook her head, but Cupie said, "Tuck loves the Raiders. Lucy said he hung this huge banner on his porch."

Chuck glanced at me. I shrugged. "Better than nothing. And nothing's all we got, otherwise. We can be there in twenty, thirty minutes, if you put the siren on."

"All right," Chuck said. "Thanks. Go back to partying."

"Is Lucy in trouble?" Leila asked.

"Not with me."

"With someone else?"

"Yeah," he said, rubbing his eyes. "I think so."

CHAPTER FIVE

Out of habit, Eddie would've kept his speed pegged at the limit anyway, but as he drove away from Tuck's place, he obeyed every speed limit sign and stoplight he came to religiously. Getting pulled over by a cop was never a good time, but with an unconscious sixteen-year-old girl in the passenger's seat, he would've been dead meat on a traffic stop.

He'd come prepared, though. Five minutes away from Tuck's, Eddie pulled over on a side street in a subdivision, choosing a lonely spot between houses. The delay made him antsy, but he needed some kind of story. He parked and hurried to the trunk, where he pulled out a blanket and an old letterman jacket.

His inclination was to dump the girl in the trunk. Roll her in the blanket, wrap the whole thing in tape, and hit the road. But this was a special situation, calling for extraordinary measures. One bruise or cut on the girl and the whole deal could be over. Not to mention, if he got stopped for any number of stupid reasons, one of the first things a cop would do is ask him to open the trunk. *Sorry, Officer. Let me just move this unconscious girl out of the way and let you get on with your search.*

No, it might be nerve-racking, but he needed the girl to be in perfect condition, so she was going in the front seat. If he could keep her doped up or even just intimidated long enough to get through the night, he might pull off the biggest trick of his career.

Eddie opened the passenger's-side door and held the girl's head as she nearly rolled out of the car. With effort, he got the blanket tucked around her, from feet to neck, then balled up the letterman jacket and slid it under her head, propping her against the door as he shut it carefully. He examined her through the passenger's-side window, acting the part of a cop looking at the same scene. With a bit of imagination, she appeared asleep, passed out drunk, or sick. He shrugged. It would have to do. All he needed was a couple of hours.

One last thing. He pulled out her phone, which he'd taken from her purse. With a stomp and a twist, he cracked open the case wide enough to pull out the thin, lithium-ion battery. A quick sidearm winged it through the woods lining the street. The rest he snapped back together and pocketed. He'd toss it as he drove. There wasn't a phone made that could be tracked when its battery was forty miles away from its working parts. He hopped in the driver's seat, closed the door—careful to use the frame, not the armrest—and was back on the road minutes after stopping.

Woodbridge was a pit, with but one redeeming quality: it was literally a mile away from Interstate 95, the East Coast's major north–south artery and chock-full of cars from Maine to Florida. He could hardly ask for a better, faster, or more anonymous route out of Virginia. With easygoing lefts and rights, always using his signal and driving smoothly, Eddie found himself on the on-ramp for the highway, where he bumped his speed up to the limit, merged with traffic in the right-hand lane, and set the cruise control. He was an economical driver, twitching the wheel a hair to avoid cracks and potholes, using deft, precise movements to pass when he needed to. Driving a highway at fifty-five was enough to drive him crazy, but better safe than sorry. Not to mention, even this late at night, there was traffic and there were morons. A few times Eddie had to slam on the brakes or swerve to avoid someone doing something stupid. He gritted his teeth, fighting to stay calm. It was going to be a long night and he needed to keep his cool.

He fell into his driving rhythm, watching idly as he flew by each highway lamppost. Cars by the dozen passed him, their red taillights twinkling in the night and leaving the afterimage of a red cat's tail. Oncoming traffic heading south was mercifully light. Headlights, especially the new blue LEDs, hurt his eyes and gave him a headache. Freeway walls the color of sandstone rose on his right, protecting the townhome communities from the worst of the noise. In the places where the highway planners hadn't bothered, malls and industrial parks lit the countryside with bright red, blue, and yellow store signs. White lamps stood sentry in the parking lots, arrayed in perfect rows for no one to see.

The crummiest strips reminded him of Carolyn Park, the bastard child of suburbia and city ten minutes south of Baltimore. It wasn't the ghetto, but it sure as hell wasn't the crème de la crème, either. That was the problem. Nobody was too low or too high. All the souls floated forever in the lukewarm soup of the lower-middle class. Life was high school football and Budweiser signs and jobs down at the shipyard. Neon "OPEN" signs were the lighthouses, guiding the faithful to the church of the Dollar Tree. Welfare checks papered single-parent homes, three-job mothers slept in basement apartments, drunks and sluts and crooks smoked together on the corner of Too Little and Too Late. That was Carolyn Park.

Eddie laughed softly and shook his head. He still couldn't hitch a verse together that didn't reek of melodrama. But he couldn't seem to leave it, either. He was a thug and a pimp and a crook, but he was an artist at heart. For what that was worth. Not much call for poets in Carolyn Park. Try telling people on Pennington Avenue about Ginsberg or Baldwin or Williams and they thought you were talking about the rookies on the Ravens' starting defensive line.

He cracked the window and glanced at Lucy to make sure the static roar of wind hadn't woken her, then deftly lit a cigarette while keeping the steering wheel on track with a knee. A deep drag filled his lungs, calming him. He held it for a long minute, then pursed his lips carefully and exhaled toward the open window. So, a would-be poet in a dying dockyard town keeps his mouth shut if he doesn't want to go crazy or get his ass beat—well, that happens anyway from a father and an uncle—so he turns all that creativity and thought and energy toward girls. And he's as good with them as he ever thought he'd be with sonnets and rhymes, but instead of reading at slams and open mics and applying for scholarships, he's writing love notes and quoting the same ten lines of Lorca memorized from a book in the library and getting laid in the back of the auditorium between periods.

But sex isn't money . . . until you make sex *into* money. Make them love you and let them think you love them back. Then they do anything for you.

Eddie held the cigarette to the crack in the window and let the wind take the ash away. He glanced at the girl. Still out cold. He reached out one long arm and felt for the pulse in her neck. If Tuck had given her one pill too many . . . but no, she was fine. Well, alive, at least. She groaned softly at the touch and her head lolled to one side. He pulled the blanket up to her chin. She was going to be sick as a dog when she came to. Roofies did that. He might as well make her as comfortable as he could.

This wasn't the life he'd planned. Then again, he'd never had a plan. Nobody in Carolyn Park did. You worked, you drank, you fucked, you died. If you wanted anything else out of life, you were either delusional or you left. Plans were almost as bad as dreams and most dreams in the Park ended right after they were jotted down in high school yearbooks or on the last page of a diary or whispered in your girlfriend's ear.

Eddie refused to dream. Dreams were a good way to make sure you didn't actually accomplish anything. But he'd had an idea once, an idle thought that he'd refined and patched and buttressed for years.

He'd make money, enough money to slip away from the life. He'd leave the girls and the drugs and the booze and he'd go north, maybe Vermont or New Hampshire or Maine. And he'd buy—no, he'd build, with his hands—a cabin. In the woods. Near a creek. It would be cold as hell most of the year, but he'd chop wood and pump water and do whatever else had to be done to stay alive on the border of the Great White North. And when he wasn't doing any of those things, he'd write poetry. Reams of it, all kinds. Sonnets and couplets and stanzas. And it wouldn't matter how good or bad it was. Poetry would simply be who he was and what he did. If it didn't get published or bought, he wouldn't care, because he'd have his cabin and his wood chopping and his poetry. And that would be good enough.

Of course, life had decided that plans weren't any good if they didn't involve a few major detours along the way. What had started out as a pretty modest desire had taken one hell of a turn a few months ago, making the whole plan seem pretty silly. And the future scary. But it was still doable, as long as he kept his head, got some help along the way, and the score was big enough—

Cop.

Eddie's pulse jumped and his mouth went instantly dry. Flashing lights, coming at him on the opposite side, south on 95. Fast. *Real* fast. A hundred? One twenty? A quick glance as it passed told him it wasn't a cruiser—it was a plainclothes car. Not your typical plainclothes, either, something sporty and low to the ground. He dropped the cigarette out the window and put both hands on the wheel at two and ten, telling himself to keep it together. He was on the other side of the highway, for Christ's sake, he was doing the speed limit, no one in the world knew where he was right now or that he had a catatonic sixteen-year-old girl in the passenger's seat.

It was gone. By the time he'd talked himself down from a panic, the lights weren't there anymore, fading from sight in less than ten seconds. He swallowed and breathed deep, then swore at himself to pay attention. A car like that . . . he never would've thought *cop*. No more daydreaming. This was real. It was dangerous.

Time to get serious. He put the window up, double-checked his speed, glanced in the mirror. He gave himself a minute and, once he felt he was in a safe stretch, pulled out his phone. Glancing between the screen and the road, he scrolled through his contacts and past calls until he found the number he wanted. He punched it and waited. It rang four times before someone answered.

"Yes?" The voice was soft and cultured.

"Is John there?" Eddie asked.

There was a pause. "I think you have the wrong number."

"Sorry," Eddie said and ended the call.

He slipped the phone back in his pocket, took a deep breath, and put his attention back on the road. But he allowed himself a brief smile. All systems were go and payday was just a few hours away. He glanced over at the girl to check on her and his heart stopped for a second time in the past minute.

Her eyes were open, glittering black, and staring straight at him.

CHAPTER SIX
THIS MORNING

"We're doing what?" Sarah asked, staring at Lieutenant Kline. "Sir?"

"The case is being handed over to the Washington County Sheriff's Office," Kline said as they walked down the corridor at the Waterloo Barracks toward their respective offices. Well, toward Kline's office and Sarah's desk in the bull pen. And at a record pace, too. Kline was over six feet tall and she had to take ridiculously long strides to keep up. "The homicide was committed south of Hagerstown and west of Frederick. You do know your counties, don't you, Trooper?"

"Yes, sir," she said. Sarah imagined putting her irritation and anger in a vise and leaning on it until the jaws clamped tight. "But the evidence that led me to the house, sir, was gathered in Frederick. And I feel like it's pointing to something bigger than any two or three sheriffs' departments can handle—"

"You *feel?*" Kline said, stopping abruptly. Caught off guard, Sarah bumped into him and backed away quickly, flushing in embarrassment.

"Refresh my memory. Was there evidence at the scene that suggested a conspiracy?"

"No, sir, but we haven't been through all of—"

"And have we had a report of any other crimes or convictions that would lead us to believe that there's more than one criminal at work here?"

"Actually, sir, I believe—"

"I think what you meant to say is *not at all*," Kline said, peering down his nose at her. His hair was shaved close to the skull, doing nothing to soften the thin, ascetic planes of his face. "Is there a rash of teenage kidnappings being reported on the TV or are teams of hookers storming the state capital?"

There was nothing to say to that.

He pinched the bridge of his nose. "Haynesworth, I'm aware of your credentials coming out of Sykesville. I know that you were the youngest trooper to get promoted to TFC . . . and without logging the requisite three years. I've seen your work, your grades, and the reports from your academy supervisors. But if you ever tell me you *feel* you should open an investigation that has me stepping on the toes of half a dozen jurisdictions, we're going to have a talk. Clear?"

Without waiting for an answer, Kline stalked down the hall with his skinny cowboy swagger, went into his office, and slammed the door. Sarah glared, then took a deep breath and peeled off in the opposite direction to the trooper bull pen.

Two out of the six desks were occupied. Jimmy Noles—two years older, but a grade below Sarah—was waiting with a look of sympathy. Aside from his expression, he was regular in nearly every way, from his average height to his average build to his brown hair and brown doe's eyes.

"You heard that?" she asked, tossing the manila folder with her notes on her desk and flopping into a chair.

"His voice carries," he said. "And, you know, this whole building is the size of a McDonald's. You can hear everything."

"Everything?"

The Wicked Flee

"It's so small, I can hear Kline take a leak. And the bathrooms are on the other side of the barracks."

"What do you think, Tom?" she asked, turning to the other trooper. Tom Cassidy was squinting at his computer. He had a shaved head and thick salt-and-pepper mustache. He ate sunflower seeds one at a time from a tall, narrow plastic bag.

"You can hear when it's Kline," he said without looking away from his screen. "He squeezes extra hard."

Sarah smiled, then got to her feet and went over to the coffeepot. Taped over the coffeemaker was a set of eyes cut out of a magazine. Tom had read that people tended to pay on-your-honor expenses more often when they were faced with an accusing stare, even if it was made of paper. Everyone had laughed at him, but the office hadn't been short on coffee and filter money since he'd stuck it there two months ago.

Unfortunately, she was out of dollar bills to put in the pot. She put a hand over the face while she poured a cup with the other. Two creams, three sugars, a quick stir and she went back to her desk, averting her eyes from the stare.

She sat down, put the manila folder to one side, and logged in to her computer. With quick strokes, Sarah put the day's paperwork in its place—answering e-mails, responding to requests, filing reports. Through it all, she could feel Jimmy watching her. She refused to look at him. He kept staring. Out of the corner of her eye, she saw him quirk an eyebrow a few times.

Without looking at him, she said, "I'm not going to look at it."

"You sure?"

"Yes."

Jimmy nodded sagely, went back to his own paperwork. A minute of silence passed, then she saw him fold his arms over his chest and tap a finger to his lips in a pantomime of deep thought.

"Jimmy, it's over. Kline said so. I'm not going to open it."

"What are you talking about?" he asked. "I'm just thinking."

She sighed, finished the last of her e-mails, then began the paperwork that would transfer the case to the Washington County Sheriff's Office.

During a fueling stop, Trooper First Class Haynesworth was stopped by a white teenage female ("TONYA BECKWORTH") at the Jessup FastGas filling station on Maryland Route 26. Ms. Beckworth told TFC Haynesworth that, several days before, a friend ("TIFFANY CHILTON") had gotten into the black Mustang of a man they'd seen at the filling station four or five times over the course of several weeks. The man had wanted Ms. Beckworth to go, as well, but she had refused. Ms. Beckworth had not seen Ms. Chilton since that time.

"How many homicides you think Washington County gets a year?" Jimmy asked into the air. "You know, the sheriff's office that's going to take on the case that Sarah broke wide open?"

"Less than one," Tom offered. He still hadn't looked away from his screen.

"Crack squad then, probably," Jimmy said, impressed. "They must have a close rate of between zero and a hundred."

Sarah shot Jimmy a withering look, which he returned with a sweet smile.

Ms. Beckworth relayed that the man in the Mustang had propositioned the girls. Ms. Beckworth refused, but Ms. Chilton agreed and left with the man. She later admitted to having consensual sexual intercourse with the man several times over the following week and that he'd arranged a "special job" for her. Ms. Beckworth described Ms. Chilton as "afraid to let him [the man] down."

Unable to investigate, TFC Haynesworth gave Ms. Beckworth her direct phone number. On January 16, Ms. Beckworth called and said she'd seen Ms. Chilton briefly with another man (not the man in the Mustang) in a blue Ford pickup. The truck had not stopped but Ms. Beckworth had been able to record the license, make, and model of the car, then called TFC Haynesworth.

A trace of the license plates led to the address of a white male (KEVIN HANDLEY). Upon investigating Mr. Handley's home, TFC Haynesworth interrupted Mr. Handley moving the body of a deceased white female resembling the description of Ms. Chilton—

Sarah slammed the mouse down and sat back, glaring at the screen, then looked over. Jimmy was watching her, eyebrows raised.

"What?" Her voice was belligerent.

"Nothing."

"*What?*"

"You know this one's connected to the others."

"Of course it is," she said.

"No bodies," Tom said, slipping a seed under his mustache.

"Why do we need a damn body every time?" Sarah asked, kicking her desk. "And who says it's murder? When did kidnapping or coercion stop being crimes? Three witnesses report a teenage girl getting into a black Mustang at the 95 Welcome Center north of Laurel. A fast-food waitress sees another get picked up outside a school near Columbia and she hasn't been in class since. Tiffany Chilton was sleeping with a guy driving a black Mustang and the next time anyone sees her, her body's being dragged through the snow in the back ass of Washington County."

"Runaways," Tom said.

"Except Tonya sees Tiffany again a week later and a mile away in a strange truck before she disappears for good?"

"Hooking."

"What if she was? We're supposed to throw her away, like she's trash?" she asked, her voice scornful. The older trooper raised his head with a hound-dog look on his face and she waved an apology. "Sorry, Tom. I know you don't believe it, either."

"So, what's the problem?" Jimmy asked. "Follow up."

"The problem, Einstein," she said, with a look of wonder, "is that my barracks commander told me to drop this or I'm going to be directing traffic for schoolkids for the rest of my career."

"You do everything you're told?"

"Yes," she said, exasperated. "It's how you keep your job. What do you want me to do, Jimmy?"

He glanced at the door, then came over and sat on the corner of her desk, leaning in. "You're at the barracks three hours a day. You respond to calls maybe four hours a day. Sometimes less. That's seven hours out of shift, which leaves one."

"So?"

"*So* . . . shave off a wee bit more and you'll have two hours a day to look into this. Run down a lead or two, knock on some doors. I could help out here or there." He pivoted on the corner of his desk. "What about you, Tom? Want to pitch in?"

Tom shot him a look, popped a seed, and turned back to his monitor.

"*He's* got the right idea," Sarah said. She squinted at Jimmy. "Why do you want me to do this so badly, anyway?"

Jimmy shrugged. "It's something exciting. A real case. I'm tired of fixing flats and scraping cars off the highway."

"So you do it."

"Not my case, chiefette," he said, sliding off her desk and walking back to his chair. "And I don't poach. It's against the rules. Besides, you're the hotshot."

"Hotshot," Tom echoed.

"Yeah, Kline gave me that impression," Sarah said, sour.

"What's he going to say when you find there's a serial killer out there?" Jimmy asked, spreading his arms wide.

"He's going to say I've got ten minutes to clean my desk out," she said. But she leaned forward and opened the manila folder. Halfway through the stack of papers she'd compiled over the past three weeks was a photocopy of a map of the north-central slice of Maryland. On it, she'd circled the locations of the three abductions—alleged abductions, she corrected herself. To that, she'd added color-coded points for any other leads she'd gathered and to which case they belonged. She traced the locations with her index finger. The three described a neat triangle.

Stop it, she chided herself, *no assumptions*. Any three arbitrary locations connected by lines always made a triangle. The shape wasn't conclusive by itself; the locations were just a component of the whole, a data point. Important, critical maybe, but far from conclusive. It was the accumulation of data that mattered. Times sticking to places, facts slotting into testimony, lies butting up against the truth.

The coincidences of the three disappearances had bothered her immediately. By the time Tonya Beckworth had approached her at the FastGas—shy, afraid, determined—Sarah had already been on the lookout for the black Mustang or girls fitting the description she'd gotten from the friends and teachers of the first two assumed runaways. Finding Tiffany Chilton's body at Kevin Handley's home had simply sealed the deal. Not an isolated murder, not a random teen prostitute with a bad ending. *These are related.*

But getting the data to prove it took effort and took time. Maybe more importantly, it took permission. *Don't go off the grid*, an instructor had told her at Sykesville. *You're part of a team. Teams solve crimes. Start freelancing and the bad guys win.* But what if it wasn't taking away from any of her regular duties? What if she did this on weekends and after hours? She was single, young, and had the time. And . . . maybe she could put in an hour here or there during a regular shift. Instead of sitting in a highway median, having the same effect on speeders as an empty cruiser parked in the same spot, she could save the next young girl from getting killed.

She raised her head from the map, her decision made, then looked across her desk. Jimmy was looking at her with a knowing smile on his face.

And he quirked an eyebrow.

CHAPTER SEVEN

Steve Torbett ended the short call and put the phone down on the desk. The phone had a piece of masking tape with "#3" written in blue ink on the back. The tape was peeling and he idly smoothed it back down with a thumbnail, working to control his excitement as his mind raced. In eight hours, maybe less, he'd have his birthday present. Not quite gift-wrapped with a bow on top, certainly, but young and unblemished. And all his.

Eddie hadn't sent him a picture, so he was left with nothing but speculation about what she looked like. Tall? Thin? Too thin? He'd demanded an Asian girl, so one could assume the black hair and dark eyes, but was the hair long or short? Had she dyed it or did it have the copper streaks that sometimes happened naturally? She'd be small-breasted, probably, but . . . what if she wasn't? Wouldn't that be wonderful? The world of possibilities excited him and made him dizzy.

"Not yet, Steve-o," he said out loud. His anticipation was like a guitar string stretched close to snapping. "You have formalities to observe first."

He opened a notebook sitting on the desk and flipped several pages to the one with #3 listed at the top, then read down the lines. There were nine entries, each meticulously recording the time and duration of a phone call. If he wrote down tonight's, it would be the tenth. But that was against the rules. With a swift, sure motion, he ripped the page out of the book, folded it, and slipped it into a pocket.

He grabbed the phone and proceeded from his office with its mahogany desk and leather guest chairs that had never been sat upon and to the kitchen where he'd never cooked a meal. The phone went into a plastic bag and thence into the freezer, then he took the piece of notebook paper and dropped it into a blender along with a banana, a cup of orange juice, and some peanut butter. He blended the contents smooth, then poured the result down the garbage disposal, leaving the motor on for a full five minutes. In another hour, he'd take the phone out of the freezer and smash it to bits on his back porch with a ball-peen hammer he kept in the kitchen for that purpose. He'd give them to Danny to distribute around the city until God himself couldn't put the phone back together.

Then he'd move on to phone #4. It should last him quite a while, since he wouldn't be making many phone calls—his gift would keep him busy for several weeks, at least. On the other hand, the rules stated that all phones were to be destroyed after a month, regardless of the number of calls. He always had trouble with that one. It offended his sense of economy to destroy a perfectly good phone, but rules were rules. And it was rules that had kept him alive and out of trouble so far.

Speaking of rules, it was time to shed some DNA.

One hundred strokes with a hairbrush, even though he had precious few hairs left these days. A thorough trim and buff of the nails (no sense in accumulating anything untoward under one's nails if there happened to be a struggle) preceded a quick body check to make sure he didn't have any cuts or scrapes that might leave a pesky blood sample behind. By the time he'd completed the DNA purge with a brisk shower, he was feeling like a new, and much less traceable, man. In reality, as precautions went, the ritual was borderline ineffective. But it made him feel in control and organized.

As he toweled off, his stomach gurgled. The suppressed sound reminded him of another task he had to take care of before he left to accept delivery of his gift. He dressed quickly, then headed to the first floor. The garage door was just off the kitchen and he went out to his black Lexus. He popped the trunk and gazed down at his Christmas present to himself, wrapped in yards of six mil clear plastic and black tape. There wasn't any movement, not now, but for some time the gift had writhed and moaned and—near the end—burbled a bit, like his stomach had. He called Danny on his cell, who came from his quarters at the rear of the house.

Torbett's records told him that this was Danny's eighth year of employment. He counted himself lucky to have found someone so sympathetic to his . . . habits. And with almost no scruples or goals of his own. At least, the blank face and unruffled black hair had never betrayed any. Torbett had his suspicions that Danny helped himself to the gifts when Torbett was done with them. He didn't mind. It was an easy perk to offer in exchange for his silence.

"Drop this in the back," Torbett said, pointing at the limp figure in his trunk. "Like the others."

Danny nodded and lifted the body out of the trunk. It was small and, with the life gone from it, seemingly light. On the way out of the back door of the garage, his servant grabbed a spade hanging on a wall and then he was gone. Torbett's property was nearly twenty acres and Danny could and would carry . . . it . . . the length of the plot without anyone noticing. It would disappear, like the others, never to be found. At least, not until Torbett was long gone. His property was fenced, electrified, and above suspicion. A mass grave was the last thing anyone would expect to find on the property of Steve Torbett, Internet millionaire. Not that anyone would be searching for the girls that were buried there. They'd already been lost to society—dead, you might say—before he'd gotten to them and no one had even noticed their absence, let alone come looking for them.

"Out of sight, out of mind," Torbett said idly. He gazed at the door for a long moment. He wondered from time to time why he did what he did and why he enjoyed it so much. He'd researched the issue in the past, attempting to analyze himself like a laboratory specimen. Poring over books and articles, he tried to understand the likes of Bundy and Jamelske and Garrido, to corner some parallel behavior to his own, to examine the evidence and make a judgment.

Did he have mommy issues? No, he loved his mother and father both. He'd never had problems of dependency or delayed maturity. Was it because he'd never had a real relationship with a woman? He had and, while they'd never developed into anything substantial, if that was an indication of insanity, half the country would've been locked up by now. Was it the media? Television was thick with news reports and docudramas about the abductions of young girls, but he hadn't found himself titillated by the reports as he was disgusted by the inefficiency and sloppiness of the kidnappers.

In a quest to find what was "wrong" with people like himself, he began with the fundamental question society always asked, which was *why are you broken?* The question had been put to other great men, but the answers had always been vague, inaccurate, and, in the end, insufficient. Jefferson owned slaves, Gauguin slept with little girls, and Burroughs killed his wife, but they were all simply "misunderstood" or "victims of their time" or, well . . . there simply wasn't an answer. Their proclivities and passions were integral to who they were and that was the end of the matter.

So, in the absence of any convincing counterargument, Torbett decided that the answer to *why are you broken?* was simply, *I'm not.*

And that had been good enough for him.

His phone beeped in his pocket, shaking him out of his reverie. Glancing at it, he was surprised to see that the noise had been his reminder to start his preparations for the night. An alarm set three hours ago, already gone. Time really did slip by sometimes.

He hurried to the door, as anxious as a puppy—he only had a few hours to get the house ready and then make the drive east to get his package. He didn't want to be late.

CHAPTER EIGHT

Patrol officer Terry Graham was heading back to the station, ready to be done with this bitch of a night.

It was cold. Cold enough for his breath to catch in his throat, cold enough to turn his skin to paper. Nine cars in five wrecks had decorated his stretch of the Beltway, the first one not fifteen minutes into the start of his shift at two o'clock. Each highway catastrophe had meant standing in the biting wind for an hour, taking down names and birth dates and complaints about the other driver.

Earmuffs, thick gloves, and a balaclava protected him against the freezing temperatures, but they also added a fuzzy layer over his senses, making him feel sluggish and removed from the situation. The accidents were almost identical to each other—a careless driver, a speeding car, and ice—which did little to relieve the unreal sense of déjà vu each time he pulled off the road to help. In one of the wrecks, blood had mixed with roadside ice, creating what one of the EMTs had called a strawberry snow cone. It was on the downhill side of the shift and Terry couldn't even laugh at the morbid joke. Being on patrol was exhausting, depressing work and there'd be just as many wrecks tomorrow. By the time he'd finished documenting the last accident, the outer part of his body felt as if it had been scoured away, leaving nothing but a scarecrow with a gun belt and a badge.

With the sun disappearing at five thirty, he spent most of his hours in the dark as well as the cold. Dark enough, in fact, that he nearly missed the Mustang that had pulled onto a shoulder north of Woodbridge. Only when he checked his rearview mirror did he see the running lights—no headlights—fading in the distance behind him. He grimaced. It was the end of his shift and he felt every minute of the previous nine hours. For once, he gave himself permission to imagine what it would be like to ignore the car and keep driving. *Oops, guess I missed one.* Guilt brought him back to reality and he sighed as he threw on his lights to turn around.

Then again, while he couldn't ignore a car by the side of the road, there was nothing wrong with hoping that the Mustang would be gone by the time he made the second U-turn. How great would it be if the driver had solved his problem on his own in less than a minute, climbed back in his car, and gone on his merry way . . .

No luck. The Mustang was still there. Terry slowed and pulled in behind the muscle car, angling the cruiser so that it would give him some slight protection from the traffic hurtling by at seventy miles an hour a few feet to his left. As his lights hit the car, however, he saw that the driver wasn't behind the wheel; he was squatting next to the passenger's side. The door was open and he looked like he was busy with his hands, like he was folding laundry. He raised his head, the face pale and oval in the bright cruiser lights, the reds and blues flashing over him like he was a sign at a carnival. He stood, but stayed where he was with his hands visible.

The guy was tall and angular, at least what Terry could make out in a quick glance. A swimmer or a junior college baseball pitcher. He wore a black peacoat, a black baseball cap, and jeans. Terry got out of the car slowly, with one hand on his utility belt, hovering near his gun, and walked to the back right corner of the Mustang.

"Having some trouble, sir?"

The guy grimaced. This close, he was older than Terry had thought, maybe mid- or late twenties. "Kind of. My girlfriend is sick as a dog and . . . well, she puked in the car. I was trying to clean her up."

Terry shuffled to his right, keeping the guy in a forty-five-degree arc to the front as he tilted his head to look in the passenger's side. There was a girl, a slim little thing with long black hair, lying back in the seat. Her head rolled from side to side in pain or delirium.

"Is she drunk, sir?"

A shake of the head. "The flu. She was staying at a friend's house and they asked me to come get her. I thought we could make it home before anything happened, but . . ."

Terry gestured to the highway thundering next to them. "No hazard lights in a black Mustang?"

The guy looked chagrined. "Sorry. It happened really fast. One second I was holding her hand, telling her to hang on, next thing I know she's yakking all over the place. I pulled over and started wiping."

Terry nodded. "Would you mind getting back in the driver's seat, sir?"

"Can I at least close the door? She's going to freeze to death."

"In a second. Sit in the driver's seat, please."

The guy complied, walking around the car and flopping down in the car seat. He watched anxiously as Terry knelt by the girl's side, wrinkling his nose at the unmistakable stink of vomit. He pulled a small penlight from his belt, then peeled back the girl's eyes, checking the irises. The girl moaned once or twice, then curled into a ball.

Terry stood, closed the door, then came around to the driver's side. "Can I see your license and registration, please?"

The guy's face rippled, but he handed over both pieces of ID without a word. Terry took them back to the cruiser and sat with the heat on high, snorting to get the smell of the girl's stomach out of his nose while he waited for the computer to run the plates, license, and registration.

Everything came back clean. Eddie Molter had priors for criminal mischief and trespassing, but they were ancient history and nothing to get worked up about anyway. Terry had possessed a bigger record than Molter's when he'd applied to the academy. The only odd thing was that all of the paperwork was for Maryland, but it wasn't a crime to date a girl across state lines. It *was* a crime to sleep with the girl if she was as young as she looked.

He walked back to the car and handed the items through the window. Molter looked at him with a curious lack of nerves. Most people who got pulled over either couldn't stop talking or grabbed the steering wheel with both hands like it was going to fly away.

"You seem pretty calm about this," Terry said, fishing.

Molter gave him a wan smile. "You drive a black Mustang, you get used to being pulled over."

"I guess that would be right," Terry said, then paused. "How old is your friend, by the way?"

"Sixteen. We met at church camp over the summer. Her parents asked us to wait until she was eighteen before we get married."

"Ah," Terry said, nonplussed. "Good for you. Anyway, everything checks out. You want me to take you to a hospital?"

"I don't think so," Molter said, glancing at the girl. "She just needs to get home and into bed."

Terry nodded, wished him well, and reminded him to put on his hazard lights next time he wanted to park on the shoulder of a highway. He walked back to his cruiser as the Mustang took off. He watched the car's taillights wink in the distance. Something bothered him, even as he sat down in the cruiser. The kid had looked too calm. But tense at the same time. Like he was on the clock and impatient to get to something.

He toyed with calling it in, chasing down more info on the car. Then he shrugged and put the cruiser in gear. He'd done what he could and it was the end of his shift on a bitch of a night.

CHAPTER NINE

The knob, unlocked, turned easily in my hand and the door opened into what looked like a kind of combination mudroom and trash alcove located probably just off the kitchen. The smell of mold and garbage was thick in the air.

An unlocked back door wasn't the first surprise of the night or even of the past five minutes, however. Topping that list was why I was willing to face arrest for breaking and entering, assault, and a whole raft of other serious charges that I knew the repercussion of only too well.

The answer was simple, of course: Chuck needed my help, he needed it now, and this was the most direct way to get the answers we needed. But it was hard for my ex-cop's brain not to tick off each of the misdemeanors and felonies I was flirting with the moment I'd opened the gate behind the dump that was Tuck's house, trespassed through the yard, and tiptoed up the rear porch to try the back door.

Logic suggested that we were also tempting fate for what could turn out to be nothing. Lucy might not be here at all, she might've never been here in the first place, or she might be sitting in the living room contentedly watching a movie with her ex, not expecting her brother and his friend to come bursting through the door like they were on a SWAT raid.

C'est la vie, I thought, trying to get average sentencing numbers for the crimes I'd committed—and might be committing soon—out of my head. I shut the door quickly but quietly to keep the cold air from alerting anyone in the house. Loud shouts coming from a few rooms away made me flinch until I realized from the canned voices that followed that I was hearing a TV show or sporting event cranked to a volume I'd never tried on my own set at home.

My alcove was separated from the kitchen by a cheap beaded curtain, which was great for me, as it let me examine the place without sticking my head in. Stinky, dirty, and unremarkable were the three words that came to mind. An old fridge with a dent and enormous scratch on the front sat in one corner. A stove with burnt food thick enough that I could spot it from the alcove rested in the other. Dishes in the sink, cans and pizza boxes on any other available flat surface. Nobody here.

I checked my watch. Chuck had told me he'd give me eight minutes to get around back and get inside. Not very generous if the door had been locked, too much time now that I'd discovered it wasn't. A quick pat, an old habit, told me my gun was in place. My arms were tingling down to the fingertips, another familiar feeling I got just before a raid or a bust.

Two minutes before Chuck's eight minutes were up, I eased back into the shadow of the alcove as a thin, redheaded guy sauntered into the kitchen and opened the fridge. I swallowed as I watched him dig around for something to eat or drink. He'd materialized out of nowhere, it had seemed. Maybe the living room was a sharp turn out of the kitchen. It was hard to tell. The exit out of the kitchen was dark and the noise from the TV covered everything else.

The kid took his time, rooting around the fridge like it was his job. I glanced at my watch. Thirty seconds. I squeezed my fists and rolled my shoulders to loosen up. The clink of a bottle and hiss of a cap coming off told me the kid had found what he wanted.

Fifteen seconds. I thought, or imagined, a thud from the other side of the house. I parted the beads with my hands, careful to make as little noise as possible, and took two long strides to close the gap with the kid.

At the same time, a crash and a deep-throated yell from the front of the house made the kid stand straight up like a jack-in-the-box, head turned toward the door he'd come through and completely oblivious to me. Until, that is, I grabbed the collar of his shirt with one hand and clamped down on his wrist with the other.

"Holy shit!" the redhead squeaked. The hand I'd grabbed was holding a beer bottle that hit the floor in a *sploosh* of foam as I twisted his wrist up behind his back in a come-along. He tried to turn his head to get a look at me while simultaneously struggling to get his arm free, but I pulled it inexorably upward between his shoulder blades until his fingers were wiggling just beneath his collar. He was flexible, I'll give him that.

"Dude, what the hell?" he said. "What do you want?"

Another colossal crashing sound coming from a few rooms away told me it was time to join the party. With a little bit of encouragement, I steered my catch toward the door, through a dining room, and into a living area that, as shitty as it no doubt was, had seen better days before Chuck had made an appearance. A huge, flat-screen TV was facedown on the floor with wires and game console controls and DVDs scattered around it in an arc. The front door was hanging by a single hinge and frigid air opened and closed a broken screen door every few seconds. Beer cans and paper plates were scattered around the room.

A tall, angular kid with a black knit cap on his head sat on a beat-up couch against the wall. His hands were steepled together over his nose like he was praying or crying, but a thin stream of blood ebbed through his hands and down onto a plaid shirt, so I was going to go with crying.

Next to him on the couch was a stocky bruiser with an already-swollen face and a trickle of blood leading from one nostril. His pumpkin-shaped head lolled on his shoulders as though it was attached with a piece of wet string. I'm no judge of appearances, and it was tough to tell through the recent damage, but it seemed to me as though Chuck hadn't done anything to hurt the guy's looks—it was a face that had started at a handicap to begin with.

I urged my man to walk into the living room, keeping him off balance and dancing in case he wanted to stage a rescue. But he seemed as beat as the other two and I dropped him unresisting onto the couch. Moe, Larry, and Curly, all in a row.

I glanced at Chuck. His knuckles were raw and red and he was breathing a little heavier than normal. Incredibly, his shades were still on even though I knew he must've landed a dozen punches to take a lunkhead like Tuck out.

"Are you okay?" I asked.

"I'm good," he said, but his face was a mask of anger and there was a little thread of crazy in his voice.

"What the hell, man?" the kid I'd manhandled said, whining as he rubbed his elbow where it had been twisted like a gum band.

"Shut up," Chuck said, his voice vicious, then turned to me. "Check the back. I'll watch these losers."

I glanced down at the guy Chuck had KO'd. With his head lolling to one side, he was definitely out of business. The other two stared back at me, wide-eyed and compliant. Chuck was safe. In fact, I was more worried about what he might do to them. "Sure."

I walked past them and down the hallway. Three bedrooms peeled off the short corridor. I stayed cautious in case there were other roomies, but the house was tiny and I was betting the three clowns out front were the only residents. The sleeping section of the abode was nothing to write home about. Clothes on the floor, bongs in the corner,

The Wicked Flee

some magazines and personal electronics on dressers and nightstands. I returned to the living room.

Chuck looked at me. "Anything?"

I shook my head. "No sign of her. Hard to say if she was here—the place is a pigsty. It would take a forensics team to be sure. Is this our man?"

"Yeah," Chuck said, then cast around for something. He spied a tallboy on the end table, grabbed it, then dumped the contents, still cold, over Tuck's head in a steady stream. Tuck groaned. I handed him the rest of the half-empty beers in the room, which he proceeded to pour over Tuck, as well. By the fourth, his eyes were open and he was snorting and hiccupping from the beer running into his eyes and nose.

The tall blond kid groaned and I could see the blood wasn't stopping. Based on the evidence, I'd say Chuck had knocked on the front door, the kid had gone to look through the peephole, and Chuck had kicked it—and the kid's nose—in. I knew from experience it was going to hurt like hell. Maybe we could win some hearts and minds with a little bit of compassion.

I signaled to Chuck to wait a second and went back out to the kitchen. The freezer had never been defrosted and so it was more like an ice cave than a food storage apparatus, but I found what I was looking for and chipped it away from the freezer's icy grip.

I went back to the living room and tossed the ancient bag of frozen beans to the kid with the broken nose. "Put that on your face." He raised it and tentatively pushed it against the bridge of his nose. I knew the pain was enough to make him pass out, but the throbbing would be down to a manageable thud in a second and the bleeding should stop . . . well, eventually.

Chuck looked over the trio. "Any of you assholes know who I am?"

"Rhee," the red-haired kid blurted. "You're Chuck Rhee. Lucy's brother."

"Straight up," Chuck said, turning his attention to the kid. "And I bet you know why I'm here, huh?"

The kid shook his head.

Tuck, his ambition bigger than his abilities, started to get to his feet, but I put a hand on his shoulder and pushed him back down without effort. "Listen," I said, "we all know Lucy was here. And you can tell from our, uh, method of entry that we're serious about finding her. So, we can spend the night beating on you until we get some answers or you can start talking and we'll be out of here in five. Now, where is she?"

"You're a cop," the blond kid said to Chuck, his voice muffled by the bag.

"Not tonight, we're not," Chuck said, then bent over him, his movement slow and measured like a snake's. His face was an inch away from the other's. "What's your name?"

The kid swallowed. "Che."

"And who's this loser?" he asked, pointing at the kid I'd pulled in from the kitchen.

"That's Ookie," the blond kid said.

"All right, Che. Ookie." Chuck said both names slowly, like he was savoring them. "I'm going to ask you once. Where . . . is . . . my . . . sister?"

"Man, I don't know—" Che started.

"He took her," Ookie blurted.

Our heads snapped around to Ookie. He looked like he was going to faint from the attention. "Who?" Chuck asked. "Who took her?"

"Some dude, man. Mean, tall. Like Lurch."

"When?" I asked.

"An hour ago, maybe," Ookie said, looking scared, suddenly realizing his good buddy Tuck would probably kill him for talking to us. But his tone said he was afraid we might kill him for not.

"Where'd he go?"

"I—I don't know, man," Ookie said.

"Tuck had her ready," Che said. I could see the pain lancing through his face and head, but the words seemed to spill out on their own. "She was doped up and waiting in his bedroom when the guy got here."

Chuck twitched when he said *bedroom*. "Details. What happened? What did they do? What was the guy driving? Where'd he go?"

In a matter of minutes, we'd dissected everything Ookie and Che knew, down to the black Mustang and a description of the guy's face. Sometime during the interrogation, Tuck became fully conscious and started swearing at them to shut their mouths.

Chuck grabbed Tuck's chin in a grip so strong that it had the tendons standing out on the guy's neck. "You don't get to tell them anything. What you get to do is tell me everything you know, right now, or I swear to Christ I'm going to start cutting parts off your body."

Tuck said something unsavory regarding Chuck's mother. Despite giving up sixty pounds, Chuck lifted Tuck off the ground and dragged him down the hall in a version of the come-along grip I'd used on Ookie. Tuck resisted, but he wasn't operating on all cylinders, and I doubt it would've been a fair fight, anyway. The two were a riot of arms and legs and punches as they stumbled down the hall.

"Chuck!" I called, then swore as he ignored me. I didn't want to leave Larry and Curly, even if they appeared intimidated and a little damaged. But I wasn't comfortable with the look on Chuck's face, either. I was stuck and had to settle for standing there, grimacing as we listened to the yells and fleshy smacks coming from down the hall. I slipped a hand under my leather coat and scratched under my holster.

"Man, are you a cop?" Ookie asked me.

"Was," I said, continuing to look down the hall. Ookie shifted in his seat as though he were going to stand and I turned and said, "Don't." I said it quiet, but dead on. I didn't need these two getting the idea that they could divide and conquer while Chuck was busy beating the daylights out of Tuck.

"Do something, man," Ookie said to me as he sank back down.

I stared at him for a second and said, "I already did. If I hadn't been along, one of you would be heading for the hospital. Or dead."

We looked up at the sound of one last thud, followed by a strangled yelp, then the toilet flushing three times in a row. Some low murmuring. Chuck came down the hall a minute later, rubbing his wrists.

"Did he talk?" I asked. "Or should I ask, is he alive?"

Chuck nodded once. "Yes to both. Let's go."

CHAPTER TEN

Waves of nausea woke her. Her body bucked, attempting to vomit, but she'd emptied her stomach already. The heaves were enough to pull her awake and no more.

She didn't want to open her eyes, but the rhythmic pulse of freeway lights and steady thrum of a car engine told her she was on a highway. Curled into a ball and lying on her right side, she tried to place herself by sounds and smell alone. Freezing air blew across her head and face, but even that wasn't enough to completely clear the smell of puke from her clothes or the tang of it from her mouth. Her head was aching and she shivered under a blanket or a heavy coat; the rough edge was touching her cheek. It was scratchy. Wool based on the wet-sheep smell, with the stink of old cigarettes lodged deep in the fibers. The smell made her stomach toss, but she swallowed three or four times in a row and managed to stifle the urge to heave. Her throat was raw from vomiting.

She opened her eyes a crack and tried to place herself in time and space. She was looking out a car window, which was halfway open, and it was night, which didn't make sense. The last thing she could remember, it had been morning and she'd been talking with her grandparents, arguing with them about something, walking out of the house. Then she was meeting . . . meeting Tuck. The next set of memories were fuzzy. She was sleeping or flying or stopping and being sick. Voices rose all around her, some deep and strange, some familiar, but the right voices came out of the wrong mouths and nothing fell into its proper slot. She'd woken once before, she was sure—she had a vague recollection of looking over at someone in the driver's seat, but was it Tuck? Her brother? Someone else? All that she remembered after that was her stomach heaving and being freezing cold before sinking back into unconsciousness.

The interior was dark leather and unfamiliar. The engine's growl was almost like Chuck's Integra that he loved so much, but more guttural and industrial. She watched out the window for a minute, hoping to catch sight of a highway sign or a road marker to tell her something, but she was slouched too far down in the seat and she watched in frustration as lamp poles and overhead trellises passed out of sight.

Lucy moved her hands slowly, easing them toward her pockets with agonizing slowness, hoping to find her phone by touch. But her shoulders moved the coat or something else gave her away.

"You awake?" a rough voice asked from the driver's side.

She froze, hoping she might fool him into thinking she'd stirred in her sleep. But the coat was yanked from her shoulders and tossed onto the backseat. The sudden blast of cold air made her gasp.

"You going to be sick again?"

Lucy curled into an even tighter ball. After a moment, she heard a small click and her window shut. The rush of air and road noise was cut off and the car became preternaturally quiet.

"Here," he said. She jumped as he nudged her. "Water. You need it."

She ignored him and he nudged her again, not as gently. "Drink it. Or I'll pour it over you."

Lucy uncurled slightly and rolled over enough to grab the bottle he was offering, but not enough to look at the man. She broke the seal on the bottle and took small sips, wincing as the cold water trickled down her throat and hit the soreness there. She drank a third of the bottle, surprised at how thirsty she was, before putting the cap back on.

"Lucy," the man said, making her flinch. She hadn't expected him to know her name. "We need to get the ground rules straight. Look over here."

Reluctantly, she uncurled the rest of the way and sat up. Everything on her ached and she bit back a groan. She got her first look at the driver. He was pale-eyed and blond. Lanky and big. In his twenties, maybe. Nobody she knew. He drove easily, with confidence, with just one hand on the wheel. Then she saw why.

In his other hand was a gun. It was gray or black, a blocky thing, longer down the butt than it was down the barrel. Her brother could've told what type it was. He raised it like it was a trophy.

"This is a modified Glock 17," the man said. "It can shoot one bullet at a time or I can empty the magazine before you can count to two. That means you're going to stay in the car no matter what. If we get stopped, you're my girlfriend and you got sick at a friend's house, so I'm taking you home. I want you to groan and act like you're too sick to talk. If you say anything more than that, I'm going to shoot whoever you're talking to, then I'm going to shoot you, then I'm going to go shoot your grandparents. That's right, I know all about them."

She was quiet, watching him as a knot formed in her belly.

"But if you do what I tell you to and follow the rules, in four hours, you'll never see me again. Easy enough?"

His Adam's apple bobbed as he spoke and he glanced from the road back to her face between every few words. Blocks of light played over his face as they approached, drew even with, then passed highway lights. Done with the gun, he tugged at his armrest and a portion of the interior door panel fell away. He slid the gun into the empty space then pushed the panel back, pounding it with a fist a few times for good measure. And the gun was gone.

"You're lying," she said. It popped out without conscious thought. He looked over, surprised, then shook his head. "Just do what I tell you."

She watched him for a minute. "Who are you? Where are you taking me?"

"You don't need to know and you don't want to know," he said.

She paused. "My brother is a cop."

His lips twitched. "Sure he is."

"Chuck Rhee," she said like he'd taught her to say if she was ever pulled over or got into trouble. "With the Arlington PD. He's looking for me right now."

"Yeah? How does he know you're gone?" the man asked. "You went and met Tuck on your own without telling your brother, right? You've probably spent the night before, or been out all night partying and your brother hasn't checked on you. What makes tonight any different?"

Lucy was quiet.

"Face it, honey. Your brother ain't looking for you and even if he was, it won't be until tomorrow. And tomorrow will be too late."

Lucy swallowed. "What do you mean?"

The man made a face. He'd said too much. "New rule. No talking."

She curled back into a ball. Despite the window being closed, she was freezing cold. "Could I have the coat back?"

The look he gave her made her shrink back in her seat. But he reached into the backseat with one long arm and pulled his peacoat forward, draping it over her like a curtain. Despite the smell, she wrapped it tightly around her, burrowing into its folds. Then she closed her eyes as tears spilled down her cheeks.

CHAPTER ELEVEN
THIS AFTERNOON

Sarah pulled out of the parking lot and made a lazy turn onto the road that would lead to the on-ramp heading west. Her foot eased forward on the accelerator until the cruiser was humming at just over forty-five miles an hour, then she flicked on cruise control and leaned back, settling in for the ride. She was about to make sure that the trek from Waterloo Barracks to the Washington County Sheriff's Office hadn't taken longer since the first pioneers crossing the Allegheny Mountains had struck westward to claim their own little slice of Manifest Destiny.

Kline had been literal when he'd said Sarah was to hand over the case to the local sheriff—not long after Jimmy Noles had talked her into doing a little moonlighting, her lieutenant had returned to the bull pen to tell her to get her gear and hit the road, taking with her not just all of the notes in her case files, but the suspect, too. She was to deliver the case lock, stock, and barrel.

As Kline swaggered back out of the room, she exchanged a look with Jimmy, who did everything but give her two thumbs up. Kline might think he was twisting the knife, but it was better than she could've hoped for. The assignment not only got her off highway patrol—always a bonus—it gave her more than an hour to grill the suspect off the books. She'd shoved the papers back in their folder and hurried down to the barracks' temporary lockup to get Kevin Handley ready for the trip.

She adjusted the rearview mirror to look at Handley now. He was a poster boy for creeps. Late thirties, three days of stubble. A doughy, sallow face. A hairline that had lost both the battle and the war against male-pattern baldness. He wore a black, waffle-quilted long-sleeve shirt that said "VICIOUS" in silver Gothic script across the chest. Bony shoulders poked up at odd angles under the shirt, incongruous with the potbelly.

Sarah had kept him cuffed and he'd shifted to his side rather than make the whole ride sitting hunched forward. The position forced him to watch the world pass by out the rear windshield. From the mirror, he looked to Sarah like a teenager being driven back to school, distraught by the indifference of an unfeeling world.

"Kevin," she called, then cleared her throat. Her voice never carried the way she wanted it to. But he'd raised his head. "Why'd you do it?"

He looked at her in the mirror for a second, expressionless, then put his head back down on the seat.

"I'm not asking so I can charge you," she said. "Nothing you say during transport can be used against you in court. I'm more curious than anything else."

He was quiet. The only sound was the thrum of the tires on the road and the occasional squawk from the police radio. She turned the volume down until it was a low hiss. The sky was overcast, bleached gray as bones. Weeks-old snow was piled in dirty brown banks three feet high along the entire stretch of highway. It was a world leached of color.

"Did you get angry at her? Did she try to run?"

Silence. Flecks of sleet dotted the windshield and she turned on her wipers. The rhythmic thumping was the perfect soundtrack to the monotony of the day.

"We know Tiffany was turning tricks," she continued. "Local girl, probably just starting out and totally clueless. We're thinking she and a friend hung around the FastGas, picking guys up and sleeping with them for a quick buck. Is that how it happened to you?"

Handley shifted, as though to get more comfortable.

"See, I'm asking because I think you're the victim here," she said, grasping at straws. She couldn't think of a single reason Kevin Handley would confess anything to her. Except, maybe, anger that he was the only one who'd been caught. No one liked to go up the river alone. "We know that Tiffany was being pimped out by a guy driving a Mustang. He sounds like the pro in this situation. Which means he should've known better than to let you meet with Tiffany at the gas station. That's how we found you, you know. One of her friends saw you and wrote down your plates. It was child's play tracking you down."

Handley sighed and squirmed in place.

"The problem is," Sarah continued, "we barely know anything about this guy or his operation. Which means he's free and clear while you're probably on the hook for murder one. He's out there, pimping more girls and making tons of money while you're going to be fighting for your life inside a Washington County prison."

She had no idea what life was like inside a Washington County prison, but even at forty-five miles an hour she would run out of time before she could pry something useful from Handley unless she shocked him into a reaction.

"It was an accident." The words were so soft, Sarah wasn't sure she'd heard him. She turned off the wipers and let the sleet accumulate.

"What?"

"She said she was nervous and hadn't done much . . . hooking . . . before," he said. "She thought that acting like it was a party would put her in the mood."

Sarah was quiet. She could see Handley's eyes flicking back and forth, remembering.

"We put on some music and she told me to turn the lights down, that it was too bright. She wanted to smoke some weed and then we started doing shots. I had some Beam and some Ronrico under the sink. It was fun. We met a few more times. I always tried to make sure it was like a party for her."

She watched him in the mirror. He wasn't in the car anymore, not mentally or emotionally, at least. He sighed again. His eyes glistened.

"That night, the night you showed up, she'd had a lot to drink, maybe popped some pills. She passed out and I started to undress her. That's when I felt her skin. It was . . . was . . ." He stopped and gulped. "She was like a piece of wood. Like furniture."

"What did you do then?" Sarah asked after a long minute, hoping to stretch the moment out.

"I freaked out. I didn't know what I was going to tell Gerry. I wasn't thinking straight. All I knew was that I had to get her out of my house. Then you showed."

"Who's Gerry, Kevin?" Sarah asked. "Is he the man in the Mustang?"

He looked at her in the mirror for the first time, his face blank. "I don't know anything about a Mustang. I only dealt with Gerry."

"Can you tell me about him?"

Handley let his head fall back onto the seat. "Gerry's a guy I knew from the mill. He worked the rollers. I was in supply. We hit it off, hung out at lunch. Drank some together. Lost track of each other after we got laid off. Then I seen him at a crab shack in Columbia. He told me he was into a new line of work."

Sarah gripped the wheel, willing Handley to keep talking. Something caught her eye and she looked in the side-view mirror. A line of traffic stretched fifteen cars behind her. She frowned . . . then realized she'd been so engrossed in Handley's story that she'd drifted out of her lane and was now straddling the dotted line. The drivers following her had been too scared to pass a state police cruiser or honk the horn and were now crawling along like they were all in a parade together, with her leading the way. Burning with embarrassment, she yanked the car to the right and put a stern, businesslike expression on her face as the passenger of each passing car looked over at her, wondering what her problem was.

"Did Gerry want you to help him out?" she asked Handley. "With the business, I mean."

"Yeah," he said, shrugging. "When he told me about it, I said no way. But he kept popping up at the bars and the stores I went to. Eventually he asked if I wanted to sample what he had."

"One of the girls?"

Handley nodded.

"And that was Tiffany?" No answer. "Kevin?"

"Yeah."

"And where is Gerry now?"

"I don't know. Probably out looking for me."

"What's Gerry's last name, Kevin?"

Handley shrugged. "Tena. Gerald Tena. He's got a place in Glenwood."

"Did he bring Tiffany to you?"

"Yeah."

Something nagged her. "Why were you at the FastGas?" There was no answer. "Kevin? If Gerry brought Tiffany to you, why were you at the gas station? You already had the girl."

There was a pregnant silence. Then, the tears that had been threatening spilled down the gray, stubbled cheeks. "I wanted to show her off."

Sarah watched the man's face for a long minute, then pushed down on the gas and headed for Washington County.

CHAPTER TWELVE

She woke a second—or was it a third?—time, thirsty and with the same headache. She couldn't believe she'd fallen asleep. It must've been the drugs that Tuck had given her. At least she wasn't puking anymore. There hadn't been anything to vomit for what seemed like hours, but that hadn't kept her body from convulsing anyway.

Lucy kept her eyes closed, wishing she were back in Chuck's Integra, like that time he'd brought her home from the hospital when she'd had pneumonia. She'd been twelve and terrified that it was all a ruse, that he was going to drive around in a big circle and take her back to the hospital where it was lonely and dark. He'd brought her Hello Kitty blanket from home and she'd clutched it to her chin, afraid, until they'd pulled into the driveway of their grandparents' home.

But there wasn't any blanket and she wasn't in Chuck's Integra. She was in a stranger's car, driving in the night, cold and clueless as to why she was even here. Wild plans for escape passed through her head, like unlocking the door and throwing herself out of the car in one quick motion. The man was obeying the speed limit, keeping the needle pinned at exactly fifty-five miles an hour. Compared to the speeds Chuck tore around at, it felt like she could practically step out and walk.

But she didn't have to be a physics professor to know that her body would be nothing but bloody rags by the time it stopped rolling. She'd tried roller blades the year before and had taken a tumble after building up some speed on the smallest hill imaginable at Gravelly Point. Even with pads, gloves, and a helmet, it had taken a month before the scabs had healed. And she'd been doing maybe five miles an hour . . . ten times that speed would kill her.

Would it be preferable to what was going to happen, though? Every so often, Chuck had tried to scare her, telling horror stories about what he'd seen on the job. She'd blown most of it off—she knew he was trying to warn her with scare tactics, and the more gruesome the story the better—but now she wondered if he'd embellished any of it. She choked down a lump that started in her stomach and rolled up to her throat. This time it wasn't nausea . . . it was fear.

Chuck had tried to give her tips, too, not just warnings. Things he'd learned in ten years as a cop. Her mind was blank. *Think, Luce!* Something about wires. *Wires? What wires?* If they put you in the trunk, pull the wires. A car with its taillights out got pulled over nine times out of ten or something like that. Whatever. That wasn't going to help her now, sitting in the front seat.

Maybe there weren't any wires to pull, but there might be something else. The idea was to attract attention, to get pulled over so she could start kicking and screaming until a cop helped her get out of this mess. She'd awoke facing the window again, so she turned her head slightly to look forward, looking for something, anything to help her.

Her eyes traced the interior of the car. Grabbing the keys was too obvious. The headlights were on the left side of the steering wheel, which meant they might as well be on the other side of the moon. Not to mention, if by some miracle she was able to reach them, he'd simply turn them on again. *Deal with what you've got*, she chided herself. *You're in the passenger's seat. What can you reach?* She imagined extending her arm in every direction, cataloging what she'd be able to touch. The radio, the glove compartment, the heater and AC—*that's useful*—the stick shift. And, right next to her, the emergency brake.

The brake? Lucy swallowed nervously. Would the brake stop the car in its tracks and throw her through the windshield? Or would it slow the car down gradually? She kind of hoped for the sudden stop—otherwise, the guy would just pull her hands away and take the brake off. And then what would he do to her?

It didn't matter. The most important thing to do, Chuck had told her, was to *fight back*. If you didn't, you were giving in, which was exactly what a kidnapper or a rapist wanted. Yanking the brake and slowing the car or coming to a complete stop on a highway would attract the attention she needed. Or she could try plan A and throw herself out of the car.

She eyed the brake. In the Integra, it was a lever in the middle of the console between the seats. Here it was closer to the driver, almost resting alongside his leg. She'd have to turn and dive across the seat to grab it. Of course, she'd have to make sure she didn't go through the windshield in case the car stopped on a dime. She didn't have her seat belt on, which was bad for the plan. On the other hand, she could also imagine having the belt on and lurching forward to grab the emergency brake, only to have the seat belt lock from the sudden movement and throw her back, plan foiled. She'd have to have her seat belt on and slowly ease toward the handle of the brake until she was sure the belt wouldn't throttle her.

She glanced at the man out of the corner of her eye. He was quiet, watchful. His head moved with small ticks in a machinelike rotation: the side mirror, the rearview mirror, the speedometer, back to the road.

She averted her eyes from the brake, as though looking at it would make it glow and give the plan away. But her eyes slid back, judging the distance, wondering how quickly she could do everything before the man tried to stop her. She was staring at the lever when the man suddenly braked and then downshifted as a merging car swerved into their lane. Her heart leapt into her throat. The movement had been automatic. His hand had moved so quickly from being on the steering wheel to wrapped around the stick shift. How was she supposed to put on her seat belt, yank the brake, and then run from the car when he could move that fast?

First things first. Obviously, he wanted her alive or he wouldn't have gone to all this trouble. They were driving on a highway at night in the winter. It stood to reason he'd want her to stay safe. *For now*, she thought, then smothered the fear that welled up inside her.

It seemed that he wanted her to be comfortable for some reason—the blanket and the jacket seemed a strange touch, but she remembered they'd been wrapped around her the few times she'd surfaced from unconsciousness. But the blanket had since slid to the floor near her feet, which gave her an idea.

Lucy cleared her throat and he glanced over at her, his pale blue eyes glassy in the dim lighting. "I'm . . . really cold. May I pull the blanket up? Please?"

He frowned, as if trying to read something in her question, then shrugged. "Sure, whatever."

When Lucy was nine years old, Cupie and Leila had talked her into going off the high dive at school. She'd never been one to give in to peer pressure, but she'd always had an analytical mind coupled with a trust for authority that had only recently started to erode. If the school had seen fit to put a high dive in, she reasoned, they expected students to live through the experience. It was unlikely they'd installed the thing in order to kill trusting students.

But she'd climbed the ladder before and knew that analyzing the situation on the ground, with the strong tang of chlorine in the air and the scratchy concrete safely under her feet, was very different from being twenty feet off the surface of the pool, looking between your toes at the water far below. She could make herself follow through, she decided, but only if she climbed the ladder, walked out onto the board, and jumped, all in one motion. If she stopped to think about it, she'd freeze and have to face the humiliation of climbing *down* the ladder. Dizzy with fear, she'd followed her own advice and was swimming up from the bottom before she was even aware that she'd jumped. Gasping as she broke the surface, she looked over at her friends standing by the side of the pool and had seen a wide-eyed awe on their faces that hadn't ever quite gone away.

She was on the high dive now.

Lucy straightened in her seat, reached to her feet to grab the blanket, then pulled it up to her chin, billowing it out more than she had to. As the blanket settled around her, she calmly reached over, wrapped both hands around the brake lever, and yanked back as hard as she could.

The world exploded in a tangle of screeching, shuddering, and bucking. Lucy was vaguely aware of the man swearing at the top of his voice as the back end of the Mustang swung around like a theme park ride. The car fishtailed out of the lane and off the road, hitting the rough edge of the shoulder at fifty miles an hour. The man yanked the wheel hard to the left and Lucy's frame of reference snapped violently in the opposite direction. Her head whipped left, then right, smacking the passenger's-side window hard enough for her to black out for a second.

Distantly, like a whisper from across the room, she realized they'd come to a stop. The whisper turned into a shout—*Get out!*—and she flailed at her seat belt, batting at the release button until the belt slipped off. She clawed at the door and it flew open, flooding the car with winter air.

Lucy tumbled to the ground, gasping as her hands hit the frozen cinders of the roadside. She scrambled to her feet and took off running, but she'd only gone a few feet when she saw that the highway was lined by a cyclone fence. She turned and headed along the shoulder, half-blind from the snow and reeling.

The Mustang made strange starting noises behind her and she picked up her pace. The analytic part of her mind was yammering at her, demanding to know why she hadn't waited until they neared an overpass or on-ramp. *You're not going to make it*, the cold, calculating half of her brain told her. *He's bigger and stronger than you. Not to mention you were stoned out of your head for hours.*

"Shut up," she gasped, pushing herself. She ran on the track team, had been working out and doing martial arts since she was too young to remember. *And I don't have to outrun him*, she told herself, sticking out an imaginary tongue at her analytic self. *I have to attract enough attention to get someone to stop.*

Her brain made a snarky comment that the way to attract attention would be to run *onto* the road, not beside it, but then subsided into a murmur as it realized that would be more suicidal than helpful. She suppressed all thought and concentrated on running. But the cold air was lancing through her chest and her legs started to feel heavier than they ever had at track practice. Pushing through the snow, she focused on an orange-yellow light far ahead that might be a traffic light or a signal for an off-ramp. She risked a glance back and felt a surge of triumph when she couldn't see the man at all. The good news gave her a boost of energy and she lengthened her stride despite the pain in her feet and the cold that was creeping along her legs.

Her whole being concentrated on moving, putting the feet down and picking them up. As long as she was running, she wasn't in that car. But the light wasn't getting any closer. Her nose was running and her hair was getting in her mouth as she dragged in a ragged lungful of air. She thought by now that someone would have stopped but she realized that she couldn't remember anyone having passed her—the road had been empty the entire time she'd been running.

When she heard the crunch of tires on the snow, she gave up. She slowed to a jog, then a walk, and then came to a standstill, shivering, as the Mustang pulled alongside her. The man got out of the driver's side, his face ugly with anger. He bundled Lucy, unresisting, into the passenger's seat, got back in, and took off down the highway.

CHAPTER THIRTEEN

"Gaithersburg?" I asked. I'm not sure why the information surprised me. I guess I'd always thought of it as just one more sleepy burg north of Rockville, another bedroom community that supplied DC with workers, tax income, and traffic. But why not? Crime occurs in the most innocuous places.

Chuck shrugged, shifted, put his hand back on the wheel. We were heading for the 95 on-ramp at sixty. At this rate, we'd be doing eighty by the time we merged. "Tuck wasn't in any shape for in-depth conversation. I got an address and the name of a motel."

I kept my mouth shut. It would've been smarter to give me five minutes with Mr. Tuck to see if I could wheedle a jot more information from him—not quite good cop–bad cop, more like bad cop and I'll-keep-my-friend-from-killing-you cop—but Chuck was of the mindset that to have information was to act on it. And maybe he was right. Every second we didn't spend chasing Lucy's kidnapper was an opportunity for him to slip away for good. If it was my daughter, Amanda, who had been knocked out and stuffed in some guy's car, I couldn't say I would've acted any differently.

"Do we have anything else?"

"He said there's a guy, don't know his name, who runs a string of girls out of the motel. Tuck got his rocks off there while he was working construction in Rockville. When the job dried up, Tuck asked around, see if there was any extracurricular stuff he could do. He probably meant bouncing or muscle work, you know. Get paid in dope and pussy. Answer came back, *not right now, but leave your number*."

"And he got a call recently?" I asked.

"Yeah."

"But not for strong-arm work," I guessed. "The guy told him he was looking for new recruits for the string and could Tuck help him out?"

"Yeah."

"And Tuck immediately thought of his girlfriend?"

"*Ex*-girlfriend," Chuck corrected me. "Couple months ago, he started slapping her around when she wouldn't put out. Lucy worked a little *ch'a gi* magic and that ended things."

"Ch'a gi?"

"Kick to the face. Tuck forgot she's a red belt in hapkido. Busted nose, black eye. Man, it was beautiful."

"Gives *breakup* a whole new meaning."

He huffed a small laugh.

"So, when Lucy wasn't ready to sleep with him," I continued, "Tuck, being as emotionally undeveloped as you can be and still be part of the human race, decides he won't be dissed."

"And the piece of garbage *sells* her to some pimp," Chuck said.

"Was this the guy we just missed tonight at Tuck's?"

"Not sure."

As we talked, Chuck squeezed the steering wheel until I thought his knuckles were going to pop through the skin. I was quiet for a minute, letting him get control. Snow had started to fall in fat flakes as big as quarters. They stuck to the car and left a wet trail as they slid down the glass of my window.

"One thing bothers me," I said.

"Just one?"

"Besides the obvious. Human trafficking wasn't my specialty back in the day, but I had to take crossover courses like everybody else."

"Yeah?"

"So, the trainers told us how the new breed of pimp wasn't the kind to beat his girls into compliance or make examples of them. These new guys are con men, talking the girls into hooking, duping them into thinking they're the ones making the decision. Doing it out of love, even."

"Yeah, happens in the gangs," Chuck said. "They found out that running girls is safer than drugs. Sentencing for pimping isn't nearly what it is for getting busted for dealing, and you can use bodies over and over again. A homie will have five or six girls on a string, all of them thinking he's going to sweep her off to Vegas and leave the other girls behind. All she has to do is turn enough tricks to make him love her just a little more and then everything will be swell."

"Even middle- and upper-class kids can be in it, though, right? Mom and dad are barely home, and dysfunctional when they are, so the kid is ripe for some guy to come around and tell her how special she is."

Chuck nodded. "Sure. Caused a big stink last year when the media found out some of the wealthiest kids in NOVA were turning tricks in mall parking lots."

"But the common denominator is that they're willing, at least on the surface. They come from a lousy home life or have a rebellious streak, maybe they're experimenting or maybe they need some emotional fulfillment they're not getting at home."

"Yeah, so?"

"So how does Lucy fit into the profile?"

"She don't," Chuck said. "I mean, she's got the rebellious thing down, sure. She can be a real pain in the ass. But she ain't mad at me or our grandparents. She ain't out to prove anything. When she doesn't want to do what I say, she tells me to go for a long walk off a short pier."

"Then what does this guy want with Lucy?" I pressed. "She's not going along with the program like some moonstruck teenager. If she kicked her boyfriend in the face for trying to force her into bed, she's not looking for love from some creep she never met before."

He pursed his lips. "It might not be that complicated. There are plenty of old-school pimps still out there, the ones who'll beat the hell out of their girls if they won't hook."

"Seems like a lot of trouble to get another girl for the string," I said. "Why not just scoop up another runaway? You can't tell me this guy can't get what he needs in Baltimore or down in Southeast."

Chuck was silent for a minute, then shook his head. "I don't know, Singer. Maybe there's something you or I never seen before."

It was an ugly thought and neither one of us said anything for a long minute. The Integra hummed along I-95, the broken white lines of the lane divider passing under us with a consistent pulse.

"Either way," I said, "it doesn't change the fact we need to find her. In fact, it changes things very little. We just need to get her back."

He nodded, tight-lipped, and pressed down on the gas.

CHAPTER FOURTEEN
TODAY, EARLY EVENING

Sarah checked her notebook again. Handley's information put Tena in a quiet, planned neighborhood in downtown Glenwood identical to hundreds like it in Maryland, Virginia, and Pennsylvania. The house sat at a regulation setback from the street and a comfortable, four-lawn-mower-swipes away from its neighbors. All of the houses in the plan were cut from the same pattern with little variation: two stories, vinyl siding, faux black shutters, and a good-neighbor fence in the back that spoke of middle-income respectability. Blinking icicle lights winked from gutters and kids' sleds. Snowmen of varying sizes and attire guarded every third yard. Not a place you'd pick as the hub for a network of pimps and prostitutes.

What's it supposed to look like? Crooks and whores and pimps were people, and they liked houses and cars and TVs like anybody else. They didn't have to fit a stereotype. The academy had entire classes on crack-dealing elementary school teachers and embezzling nurses who skimmed from the hospital budget. But she couldn't shake the weird image of Tena hooking up johns while working the grill at a neighborhood barbecue.

In reality, it probably all happened online. Chat rooms and forums had replaced street corners a long time ago. And that meant that the business could go anywhere, be anywhere. Take away the need to drive to a seedy neighborhood, toss in the runaways or unloved teens that existed everywhere, and stir with the never-ending supply of sleazy men with erections and money. The result? Ward Cleaver running a string of girls out of a single-family home in Glenwood.

Sarah glanced at her watch. Getting Handley to talk had been a godsend, but she had an hour at most before she had to start her regular patrol. If Kline caught her working solo on Tiffany's case a few hours after telling her to drop it, she might as well tender her resignation now.

She got out of the cruiser and hitched her gun belt higher on her hips as she walked to the front door. Her eyes played over the front of the house, hoping to learn something from simple observation, but the home was as unremarkable as every one of the buildings around it. Snow and ice had been left to pile up on the walk, while the blacktop driveway leading to the garage was clear. All that told her was that Tena drove everywhere, that the garage had a door to the house, and that her pants were going to get wet, since she couldn't exactly knock on the garage door.

No holiday decorations, she thought idly. Didn't mean anything. Only half the houses in the neighborhood had remnants of Christmas and New Year's ornaments on them. Not everyone was Christian, and not everyone liked Christmas. Sarah rang the doorbell and rapped on the door. A shadow moved on the other side, visible through the glass side panes, then disappeared without answering. She rang the bell and knocked again. A larger shadow replaced the first and the door opened.

Tena, if it was him, was big, maybe six two, with round shoulders and a beer gut that pushed out a striped dress shirt that had been tucked into black jeans. A thick, dark mustache flecked with gray made a pale, round face even paler. A gold chain—bought by a younger, thinner man—was stretched tightly between two folds of his neck. He cracked the screen door.

"Can I help you?" he asked.

Over his shoulder, Sarah could see a girl, long black hair, peeking around a corner of the living room. Tena noticed the direction of her gaze and turned to look. The girl vanished before he'd finished turning his head.

"Are you Gerald Tena?"

"Yes. What's this about?"

"Trooper Sarah Haynesworth," she said, flashing her badge. She wasn't thrilled to give him her name in case he called the barracks, but she had to demonstrate her authority to ask him questions. "Do you know a Tonya Beckworth or a Tiffany Chilton, Mr. Tena?"

He shrugged, shook his head. "No, I'm sorry. Should I?"

"How about a Kevin Handley?"

"Yeah, I know Kevin," he said. His breath steamed in the air. "We used to work together at J&L."

"Have you seen him recently?"

"Once in a while. At bars, the grocery store, that kind of thing. We don't hang out or nothing. Why?"

"Kevin Handley is in the custody of the Washington County sheriff right now," Sarah said, being careful how she said it. "He was caught last night dragging a teenage girl's body into the woods. The girl was Tiffany Chilton."

Tena's mouth fell open. "Holy crap. Did he kill her?"

"We don't know. She might've OD'd. But he's at least guilty of felony obstruction."

"Sorry, Officer. I don't know anything about that," Tena said, sounding shaken. "Kevin and I were drinking buddies at best. I haven't seen him in a couple weeks, honest."

"That's funny," Sarah said. "Because he said he'd met you a few days ago. In fact, he said you introduced him to this girl Tiffany."

Tena's face rippled and blanched, but he kept his composure. "If he said that, he's lying. I don't know any girl named Tiffany and I sure as hell didn't set him up with her."

"Are you married, Mr. Tena?"

He blinked. "No."

"Who is the girl who came to the door just now?"

"My niece. Visiting from Houston."

"May I speak with her?"

Tena shook his head. "You got a warrant?"

"For what, Mr. Tena?"

"For anything, that's what," he said, his voice getting more confident and offended. "I don't like you trying to pin anything on me. If Kevin Handley killed some girl, that's on him. He always was a sad little creep, but he ain't my problem."

"I just have a few more questions," Sarah started. "Can someone verify—"

Without another word, Tena took a step back and shut the door in her face.

Sarah stood there for a second. "That ends the interview," she murmured, then turned and trudged back through the snow to the sidewalk, doing her best to place her feet in her previous footsteps to limit the damage to her pants. Out of the corner of her eye, she saw the blinds in the front window snap shut. She sensed Tena on the other side, watching her.

The car was warm and Sarah sat, letting the heater do its work. And why not let Tena sweat a little at the same time? He didn't know she had to leave in less than five minutes and would have to push the car to ninety to make it on time.

Sarah chewed her lip. Had she handled this the right way? Tena had been nervous, but was he any jumpier than anyone else after being told that someone they knew had been caught with a dead body? And had said they were complicit in the death? Most people would react poorly, to put it mildly.

She swore. If this were a real investigation, she would've been able to put a tap on his phone and watch how he scrambled after she'd dropped the bomb on him. As it was, all she managed to do was freak him out in time for her to leave. Unless she'd managed to shock him into admitting his role in Tiffany Chilton's death, this was a dead end.

After several minutes had passed and he hadn't run out of the house with a signed confession, she bowed to the inevitable. She could tighten the screws all she wanted, but if he hadn't budged by now, there was nothing she could do about it. With a sigh, she put the cruiser in gear, made a long, slow pass in front of Tena's house, and left.

CHAPTER FIFTEEN

Eddie traced the outline of the bump where he'd smacked his forehead on the car frame. The lump was the size of a large jelly bean and hurt like hell, but he couldn't stop playing with it. Indented in and around the skin of the bump was a design that described a perfect negative of the plastic insulation around the window. His fingers returned to explore the unfamiliar bumps and contours that were now part of his body.

The crazy bitch had come close to punching both of their numbers right there on the Beltway. He'd nearly blacked out when she'd yanked on the emergency brake. Admiration warred with a deep desire to beat her senseless. Besides almost killing them both, she'd no doubt done a couple thousand dollars' damage to the Mustang. But none of the girls he knew had the brass to even think about what she'd done, let alone go through with it.

He took a deep breath. His nerves were close to unraveling. Strange rattling noises were coming from the Mustang's chassis. Going the speed limit was slow torture when all he wanted to do was pound the gas and get things over with. And he still couldn't tie Lucy up for fear he might get pulled over again, but now he had to watch her out of the corner of his eye in case she decided to do something different but just as insane as her first stunt.

"What are you going to do with me?" she asked, interrupting his thoughts. "Where are we going? Who are you?"

"I'm the guy who needs you to be quiet and not move," he said. "So sit back and relax."

"How am I supposed to do that?"

He shrugged. "There's nothing you can do, so why not enjoy the ride?"

"Because you kidnapped me, that's why," she said, her voice rising. "What do you want from me?"

"I want you to shut up."

"That's not good enough," she said with false bravado. "I need to know what you're going to do with me."

"You could keep talking and see if I'll knock your teeth out," he said.

"You're not going to do that," she said, surprising him. "If you were going to hit me, you would've done it already."

He grimaced. So she'd caught on. Smart kid. But he had to regain some control over her. It was going to be a long drive if she felt she had some leeway with him. "There're other ways to hurt without hitting."

The implied threat did the job and she went quiet again, curling into a tight ball and pressing herself back into the seam between the passenger's seat and the door.

His phone buzzed and he pulled it out to find a text from Gerry. *Call me. URGENT.* Eddie swore and slipped the phone back in his jacket, considering. He should ignore the message. Gerry was a whiner and had a hard time following the simplest of directions. But he usually communicated in rambling, nonsensical texts, e-mails, and phone calls. The very fact that he'd only sent three words made it more likely that there was a situation worth Eddie's attention.

There was a ninety percent chance that it was Gerry being his typical screwup self. But if there was even the *hint* of a possibility that he was in some kind of hot water that could be traced back to Eddie, he had to know.

He made a noise somewhere between a sigh and a groan. The choices were to call Gerry now . . . or wonder if he was on every cop's radar in a five-state radius. He couldn't afford to call while he was driving—he wasn't going to give Lucy another chance to yank the brake again while he was distracted talking to his number one pimp. A second time would probably kill them both. Or rip the guts out of the Mustang and then the whole gig would be done.

He started looking for an exit. He needed a parking lot, some place dark where he could keep a low profile for five minutes. He'd call Gerry, find out what his lame ass wanted, solve the problem for him, then get back on the road. A short detour. Unfortunate, but necessary.

It was another quarter hour before an exit came along. A highway sign directed him to a half dozen restaurants and gas stations within a few miles, but he was looking for something with more privacy. A handful of rights and lefts later, he pulled into the sterile white light of a bus stop kiss-and-ride lot. He eased the Mustang into a far parking stall and shut off the car, then turned to Lucy.

"I have to make a call. You're going to sit here and keep your mouth shut. I'm going to stare at you while I talk. If you make one move to open the door or honk the horn or do any other thing, I'll drive you to an empty lot and fucking kill you. I don't want to do that, but I'll do that rather than go to jail. Understand?"

She nodded, cowed. He slipped the phone out and hit Gerry's number under speed dial.

"Eddie?"

"What do you need, Gerry? I told you not to call today of all days."

"We got a problem," Gerry said.

"What kind of problem? One of the girls kick you in the nuts when you tried to screw her?"

"A cop came by today."

"A cop?" he repeated stupidly. His stomach reached for his feet. "What for? What'd he want?"

"She. A lady cop. Maryland state trooper."

"Okay. What did *she* want?"

Gerry took a shaky breath. "One of the girls OD'd on us when she was with a john."

"What? Who?"

"Tiffany."

"Shit," Eddie said. He could see the girl's face. He'd just put her on the string a few weeks ago. "Where'd they find her?"

"Kevin—the john—got caught trying to bury her in the woods, the dumb shit."

"And he gave you up to this cop?" Eddie asked, his mind racing as he thought about the implications.

"It must've been him. It's the only connection."

Eddie frowned. "How'd he know what to tell her? He didn't pick up Tiffany at your place, did he? I told you, never do that."

"No, no, nothing like that," Gerry said. "I . . . I knew this guy. From before, when I worked at J&L. He already knew where I lived. He's this lonely schmuck, lives near the state park. I figured we could make him a regular."

"What did you tell the cop?"

"Nothing, Eddie. I mean, even though she was here, it seemed like she was fishing, you know? Like she had my address and nothing else."

"She knew your name?"

"Well, yeah. But that's it. She asked a couple of questions, I kept my cool, and then she took off. Didn't have a warrant or anything."

"She say if she was coming back?"

"No. But she said the sheriff's office was taking over and they're a bunch of morons. It's probably going to stop with Kevin, especially if they just call it an overdose."

Until they get you to talk, too. Eddie blew out a breath. "Okay, Gerry. Sit tight. Don't go anywhere or give them a reason to bust you for something minor. If they come back and want you for questioning, you gotta go, but don't give them anything. They'll have to release you in twenty-four."

"Jesus. Eddie, I don't know—"

"Keep it together, Gerry. If they really are fishing, they'll try to spook you so you'll cop to something you didn't do. In the meantime, I'll work on getting a lawyer in case they want to push this."

"What about the girls?"

"Are they at the Crowne?"

"Yeah," Gerry said. "Business as usual."

"Good. Don't call any of them or go out for the take. I'll pick them up later myself."

"What do you want me to do in the meantime?"

"Don't go anywhere. If the cops catch you hitting the road, they might think you're a flight risk and pull you in. Got it?"

"Got it. What do we do in the long run?"

"I'm heading your way right now. We need to get you a lawyer in case things get heavy. We'll talk when I get there."

Gerry sighed. "Thanks for looking out for me, Eddie."

"No problem, bro. Keep your head on straight. I'll be there soon."

Eddie ended the call and sat for a second, closing his eyes briefly. He saw his world going black, a future being shut down before it even began. And it would, if he let it. But if he asserted himself and stepped in to protect that future, he could keep the road open. If he had the guts.

His eyes snapped open and he looked over at Lucy, who was looking back at him with her own dark eyes. His future—in the shape of this young girl—was sitting right here, but it could be taken away in a heartbeat by inaction. He had to be decisive, but he also had to protect what he had. She couldn't go with him, so he had to get rid of her. He had to stuff her somewhere safe, do what he needed to do, then pick up the pieces and forge ahead.

An idea occurred to him and he weighed it in his mind. It wasn't the best possibility, but not the worst, either. It would have to do. He turned the key in the ignition, pulled out of the parking lot, and headed for Glenwood.

CHAPTER SIXTEEN

"Tell me about her," I said.

My voice was loud in the little car. Except for my constant sniffling, we'd been quiet for twenty minutes. I'm sure Chuck was going over nightmare scenarios in his head, unable to stop the looping of the mental tape that would explore the worst possibilities, examine them, follow them to some terrible conclusion, then rewind and start from the beginning once more.

Knowing that, I normally would've embarked on some empty chatter to keep Chuck's mind from imagining the worst, but I was running a fever, operating on three hours of sleep, and had a healthy dose of cold medicine wreaking havoc with my social cues. It had taken most of my powers of concentration to get this far.

"Shit, Singer. I don't know," he said. "Typical sixteen-year-old, I guess, but what do I know about teenage girls? She runs track, does martial arts, hangs out with her friends. Does well in school. Tuck was the only big mistake she's made since I can remember."

"And she lives with your grandparents?"

"Yeah."

"It's funny. You and I have known each other for a while but I've never asked you about your . . ." I hesitated, at a loss for words. That green syrup I'd gulped down was *really* screwing with my touch.

"Family situation?" Chuck filled in for me.

"Yeah."

He sighed and pressed back in his seat. "My mother's family is from Kosong, in North Korea. When she was eighteen, Mom made it across the DMZ by some miracle, then headed south to Seoul looking for work. She didn't want to go too far since she'd left her parents behind. Wanted to try and bring them over. North Korean policy on defectors has always been to punish the ones who are left."

I nodded to keep him going. The ribbon of highway and highway streetlamps, their light muted by the snow, was hypnotizing.

"She worked in Seoul for two years. Found a few cleaning jobs here and there. Tough going. No education past high school—and North Korean school, at that. Getting an A in Communist Indoctrination don't prepare you for real life, you know?"

"How'd she get along with her new neighbors?"

"Alone. No family. No love lost with the locals. A foreign national from a shitty neighbor to the north."

"That's being behind the eight ball," I said.

He nodded. "Then she met my dad. American. Had a job at the State Department. He thought she was swell and got her pregnant. I came along and made things a little awkward, since he turned out to have a wife and nine-year-old daughter waiting for him back in San Diego."

"Oops."

"Yeah. We didn't find that out until later. He was in love and Mom worked on him day and night to get my grandparents out of Kosong. It took five more years, but he pulled some strings or laid out some serious cash and one day our little apartment had two old people living in it I'd never met before."

"When did you come here?"

He shook his head. "It took forever. Dad had made a hell of a mess with the whole 'I'm already married' thing. Had to come back and get a divorce back in the States or I would've grown up to become a cop in Seoul, not Arlington. We moved to the States . . . maybe two years after we got Grandma and Grandpa over the line."

"Tough?"

He shrugged. "Not easy. I was almost seven, so I had friends. Seoul was all I knew. You know, leaving the stuff that's important to kids hurts you at the time. But I knew English from my dad and from going to the expat school, so language wasn't a problem, at least. I stayed fluent in Korean because my grandparents don't know anything else."

"So . . . your dad got a divorce and then your parents waited to have Lucy?"

"Yeah. The divorce was messy and I think maybe Dad was regretting the way things had gone. Probably wasn't too eager to have a second kid—it would've reminded him of that sharp left turn he'd made in his life. But one thing led to another and Lucy came along when I was twelve."

"Pretty weird for you?"

"Oh, yeah. I was already an angry Goth teen in the making and a little sister didn't help." He laughed, remembering. "Half-Korean kid with an accent, wearing eyeliner and a black trench coat. Reading Japanese *manga* on the bus because no one would talk to me. Jesus. I had no idea what I was or what I was doing."

"Then what happened?"

"Ah, the typical deal. I started hanging out with the wrong crowd. Dad saw the way I was heading and stepped in early. He signed me up for a boxing class—can you see it? I weighed, like, ninety-two pounds in ninth grade—and dragged me to the gym after school. I hated every second of it."

"Couldn't have been a total waste," I said. "I saw what you did to Tuck back there."

"Well, one day the instructor made me spar with this kid named Chops. I don't know his real name, we just called him Chops. Can you guess why?"

"He told you he was gonna bust your chops?"

"You got it. I think he heard it on a cartoon or something. Anyway, he was a big kid, and slow. His only tactic was to push you into a corner then pound on your ass until you started crying."

"Sounds like a great way to build character."

"Yeah. So, the bell rang and he started bulling his way in like he always did, but I decided this time I was tired of it. I closed my eyes and started throwing punches as fast as I could. Missed most of them, but I flailed so much that I still connected ten times and he went down like a sack of shirts. Coach stepped in and stopped me before I could beat poor old Chops into mush. Dad never had to force me to go back."

I chewed on that, looking out at the blurry night for long minutes before continuing. "Fast-forward some. If you're twelve years older than Lucy, you didn't grow up with her."

He shook his head. "Nah. We got close when our parents died, though."

I grimaced. "I'm sorry, Chuck."

"S'okay. It's been a while."

"What happened?"

"They got T-boned by a drunk out near Herndon. I was seventeen, Lucy was just a little girl. They'd gone out for a dinner together. First date night they'd had in a year. Just bad luck."

I was quiet. "That what made you want to become a cop?"

After a minute, he took a deep breath. "Probably. I mean, I'm not Batman or anything—it's not like they were murdered and I dedicated my life to avenging them. The killer was just somebody who should've never been driving. But, still. Made me want to do something positive, you know?"

"How'd you cope? How'd she cope?"

"I went into the academy the next year, Lucy moved in with our grandparents, and life went on. I'm like her half uncle, half brother. I bail her out when she does something stupid, chew her out when she does something dangerous, and let my grandparents handle the rest. I figure they did a decent job with my mother. Old-world Korean values and all that."

I approached the next question delicately. "Your dad was American, but your last name is Rhee . . ."

"Yeah. Dad and I had our issues. And I've always felt American, you know, but somehow I identify as Korean." He gave a little laugh. "Hell, I don't know. It's complicated. I made the choice and I'm not even sure why. It was easier for Lucy. My grandparents became her guardians, so her keeping the name made more sense."

The miles had melted away while we talked. I watched as we passed green Beltway signs listing the major towns along the Northern Virginia corridor: Springfield, Annandale, Fairfax. If I could've seen through the trees and buildings and developments to our right, the Capitol and the Washington Monument would be shining bright and clean in the distance. Tysons, McLean, the Virginia state line were fast approaching.

Despite the hour, traffic increased as we came down the hill to cross the American Legion Bridge, ten lanes spanning the Potomac River splashing rocky and wild a hundred feet below. Traversing the bridge brought us to Maryland and we left I-495 behind as it peeled away to the east to complete the great arc of the Capital Beltway. Our path was north. If the greater DC area was a clock face, we were following I-270 as it shot away from the city at eleven o'clock on the dial. Cars merged and exited the arteries branching off to the twins of the Virginia towns we'd passed earlier: Bethesda, Rockville, and, eventually, Gaithersburg.

"I haven't been here in a while," I said.

"Can't cross the river, huh, Singer?" Chuck said, smiling.

"Hey, man, I crossed it every day and night for thirty years. Just, you know, into the city, not up here in Yahoosville."

"It's all the same. Just different license plates," he said, then pointed. "Here we go."

Chuck smoothly joined the local lanes, then took the second exit for Gaithersburg. Off-ramps and transitional roads did their job and we'd slowed to a respectable suburban speed less than a minute after leaving I-270.

"You know where you're going?" I asked.

Chuck fished around in a pocket for his phone. "No. But this does." With the ease of long practice, he drove while navigating the phone's tiny map.

I'd been to Gaithersburg only a few times before—it had been outside my jurisdiction, after all—and it wasn't such a little hamlet anymore. In fact, it was on its way to becoming a small city. Tower apartments had replaced sleepy two-story duplexes, and whole stretches of road were nothing but the neon lights of the fast-food joints, shoe stores, mattress emporiums, and pharmacies needed to serve a burgeoning population.

"What is this place and what did they do with Gaithersburg?" I asked.

"Progress, man," Chuck said. His face was lit a ghastly white from the glow of his phone. "The I-270 technology corridor plus lobbyists plus a solid housing market means suburban sprawl."

"Golly," I said, looking out the window like a hick on his first trip to the city.

Chuck took the turns with confidence, but I knew he was getting keyed up, because *I* was—a tightening in the pit of the stomach, that electric energy that I couldn't quite shake out of my hands and fingertips. In fact, I wasn't sure how Chuck was keeping his cool. If it had been me, I would've driven the car in a straight line to the address, plowing through anything between me and it.

Ten minutes later, hovering on the edge of Gaithersburg, we stopped at a street corner that gave us a view of the Huntington Crowne Motel. It looked like the kind of place a pimp would put his girls. Beat down, drab, a runner that could barely finish its race. Snow fell in clumps, piling in unplowed drifts in its modest parking lot. Streetlamps flickered on and off, but the lights in several of the units burned constantly.

I glanced over at Chuck. "Time for some direct action?"

He nodded. "Hell, yes."

CHAPTER SEVENTEEN

"Get out."

Eddie grabbed Lucy's arm and pulled her off the seat of the Mustang. They'd parked in the driveway of a small, one-story house built on a rise. Dominating the front yard was a fifteen-foot inflatable Santa Claus, lit from within by a small bulb. An odd, homemade cardboard crown had been put on its head, but the crown had gotten soggy and now drooped over the puffy face like dreadlocks. A dog barked in the distance, its voice carried unnaturally far on the winter air. It was the only sound except for a low whine from the air compressor that kept the giant Santa inflated.

The lot was surrounded by trees like every home she'd seen on the drive into the neighborhood, if that's what you could call a scattering of houses along a deserted road. They'd made a dozen different turns after exiting the highway near Glenwood, passing through the suburbs and on to the sparsely populated countryside in between towns. Lucy had gotten lost minutes after they'd left the highway.

A light came on inside the dumpy house, followed by a bare bulb that served as a porch light. The door opened and a thin man stepped onto the porch dressed in a T-shirt and jeans. He was bald back to the middle of his head and the skin of his scalp gleamed in the light. Pale arms poked out from his sides, the elbows sharp and the forearms covered with dark hair. He looked down at them, squinting into the darkness.

"Eddie? Is that you?" the man called.

"Jack," Eddie said. With a hand under her elbow, he led Lucy to the rickety, sagging steps that rose to the small porch. "How you doing?"

"Can't complain," Jack said, eyeing Lucy as they climbed the steps. "Who do we have here?"

"Mind if we come inside first?" Eddie asked. It was less of a question than a demand.

"Aw, hell. Where are my manners? Of course, of course." Jack danced back like a jester, holding the screen door open for them.

They entered and moved to one side so Jack could shut the door. The living room was small, dominated by shaggy beige carpeting and faux pine paneling. A large print of a wolf pack with picturesque mountains in the background hung on one wall. The edge of a hole peeked out from behind it. Weak light emanated from a small table lamp, the base of which was a knight holding a lance. Poorly mounted shelves took up most of the available wall space, each cluttered with dusty bric-a-brac: cheap resin figurines of castles and wizards, crystal and prisms and ordinary rocks, a needlepoint pillow with a shield and rampant lion design. A map of Britain, littered with ornate, illegible lettering and heraldic shields, hung on the wall above a nappy green couch with a seat so low that the front of it touched the floor. The couch was square to a TV, from which a loud huckster's voice hawked the latest irresistible offer. Jack snatched at the remote lying on the couch and turned off the TV.

"So," he said, tossing the remote back onto the couch. "What can I do for you, Eddie, old chap?"

"I need a favor," Eddie said. He pointed. "This is Lucy. I need to stash her here for an hour or two, tops. I've got some business that can't wait, but I can't have her . . . acting out in the meantime. That's where you come in."

"You'd like me to provide sanctuary for this young lass, yes," Jack said, scooting closer and giving Lucy the once-over. She winced as he stuck his face in hers. He smelled like garlic and jelly.

Eddie shifted closer and put a hand on Jack's shoulder. "Nothing is going to happen to her, Jack. I want her in exactly the same shape as I'm leaving her. *Exactly* the same shape. You understand?"

Jack's face fell. "Not allowed to play?"

"No."

"I hate to seem venal, lad, but what's in it for me, then?"

Eddie reached into his jacket and pulled out a wad of bills. He counted off four fifties and handed them to Jack, who took them delicately between thumb and forefinger, then slipped them into a back pocket.

"You get two more when I get back, if she's conscious, happy, and untouched. If she isn't, you don't get the money and you get me in a piss-poor mood. What do you say?"

"Not much choice you leave me, boy-o."

"I can take her somewhere else . . ." Eddie began.

"Oh, no. No, no, no. She'll be my guest. My liege lady, my princess without a pea. You have my word of honor."

"I don't need your word of honor. Just lock her in a room until I get back. That's all I'm asking."

"And it shall be done," Jack said, bowing low and sweeping his arm back with exaggerated courtesy. He turned to Lucy. "Would m'lady care for a cup of tea before I lock her in her tower? I have a nice tin of Earl of Grey that I picked up on clearance last week."

Lucy shook her head. Jack shrugged. "Suit yourself."

"Where's Doris?" Eddie asked. "I'd feel better if you were both here to watch her."

"Out for the evening, sire. She left me in charge of the freehold in her absence."

"She's out boozing with the girls from her bowling league?"

Jack inclined his head. "The same. I am left to entertain myself with the dubious charms of reality television while my wife frolics with her court."

"Call her. I want her here."

"But I am perfectly capable . . ."

Eddie reached out and put his hand on Jack's shoulder again. This time, however, he slowly squeezed, pinching the thin muscle in Jack's neck. Eddie seemed to put little effort into the motion, but Jack gasped and his knees buckled. He put a hand on Eddie's, ineffectually attempting to pull it away.

"Jack, I don't think I'm being clear," Eddie said, his voice even and conversational. "This is important."

"Okay," Jack said hoarsely. "Okay. It's serious. No fucking around."

Eddie maintained the pressure for a few more seconds, then let go. He stared at Jack. "Call Doris and get her back here."

"I . . . I don't have the phone tonight," Jack said, humiliated.

Eddie closed his eyes briefly, then said, "Give me her number. I'll call her." Jack recited it and Eddie punched it into his phone. "I'll be back in an hour, maybe two. Got it?"

"Got it, Eddie," Jack said, subdued.

"Good." Eddie turned to Lucy. "Do what he says. Don't try to run. We're in the boonies, so there's nowhere to go anyway. You heard what I told Jack. I'll be back in an hour. Don't make any trouble."

Lucy stared at the floor. Eddie gave Jack one more warning look, then he opened the door to a blast of freezing air, and slammed the door. A minute later, the rumble of the Mustang's engine shook the pictures on the wall, then the headlights played over the front of the house as he backed out of the drive. With a roar, the muscle car dropped into gear and took off down the road and away, the sounds of the engine eventually fading into the distance.

Humming to himself, Jack peered out the front window until the last sound of Eddie's car had died away. Lucy jumped as Jack spun in place and clapped his hands together loudly.

"All right, my girl," he said with a grin. "It's just you and me. What say we get to know each other better?"

CHAPTER EIGHTEEN

Torbett was stepping into his Lexus when #4 buzzed once, twice. He pulled the phone out and frowned. A Virginia number. Eddie. He hesitated. *Three rings.* Two communications in the same night was dangerous, against the rules, definitely verboten. As Eddie should know. *Four rings.* But the consequences of ignoring a call were potentially severe, possibly even disastrous. Eddie might've lost the girl. Or maybe he'd changed his mind and Torbett had almost made a huge mistake. *Five.*

"Damn," he said. He pushed the little green button. "Hello?"

"John? We need to talk." Eddie's voice had a distant quality, as though he were talking on a speaker.

There was a problem. Back out. "I'm sorry. I think you have the wrong—"

"Don't hang up. You're safe. I know you throw the phones away. You need to hear this."

A wave of panic at the idea of a good plan possibly gone awry washed over him, or worse, that perhaps the walls of the legal system were closing in at this very moment. Another section of his brain, however, registered peevish disappointment. He'd taken time cultivating

Eddie, getting to know him before entrusting him with an order. The boy had seemed the reliable sort. Someone, perhaps, he could do repeat business with (although that was flouting the rules). But if there was a problem serious enough to call him twice in a night—in fact, if he needed to call him at all, and not simply handle the issue himself—it was doubtful that Eddie was the man he'd hoped he was, after all.

"You have one minute," Torbett said. "Then I'm ending this call and our relationship."

"Relax. You're not in any danger. I've got a problem on my end that doesn't involve you, but it's something I have to take care of before I deliver the package. It means a one-, maybe two-hour delay."

Torbett was silent.

"I called so that you wouldn't be waiting any longer than you have to," Eddie said, his voice reasonable, soothing. "I know you want a minimal amount of contact at the drop-off and I'm trying to provide that for you."

Torbett cleared his throat. "What's the problem?"

"You don't really want to know, do you? It's nothing that involves you. No one knows your name or anything regarding our arrangement and you don't know anything about my end of things. That changes if I tell you."

"This doesn't involve the police? You're not posting bail or anything?"

Eddie's chuckle was made metallic and disembodied by the distance, like a ghost's laugh. "No, John. Nothing like that."

"It makes me jumpy, thinking you have other priorities."

"Believe me, this isn't more important than delivering your . . . product. It's just an unpleasant surprise. If I could ignore it, I would."

Torbett chewed it over. "All right. What do you want me to do?"

"Wait two hours and follow the schedule just as we agreed. I'll make sure the timing works on my end. Everything proceeds as planned. Next to no contact, a safe handoff, then we go our separate ways. As long as you have the delivery fee."

"Fine. We'll stick to the plan," Torbett said. "This makes me nervous, though. I'll be getting rid of this phone as a precaution. You have the next number in the chain in case you have to call again?"

"Yes."

They ended the call and Torbett sat in the dark, thinking. The swell of panic had subsided. He'd imagined Eddie calling for all kinds of terrible reasons, but this had been nothing, really. Troubling, yes. An inconvenience, certainly. But nothing catastrophic. He'd put Eddie on probation after this, however. It wasn't a failing grade, but definitely a black mark for the future.

He sighed, got out of the car, and went back into the house to go through the ritual of destroying yet another phone. *Adieu, number four. I hardly knew you.* After he put the phone in the freezer, he put it out of his mind to deal with later and went down the hall to the study. He opened the drawer in his desk and pulled out the next phone. *Bonjour, number five.* He slipped the phone into his pocket, then blew out a breath and looked around his office.

How to kill two hours?

He turned and knelt by the safe that was embedded in the wall behind the desk. With a few quick turns of his wrist, he unlocked the vault and opened it. Inside were papers and some cash, a handgun that he'd never fired, and a stack of generic photo albums that he'd bought at a department store. He shuffled the albums, checking the names and dates handwritten on the spines, then picked one at random. Sandy, last year's Fourth of July gift to himself. He poured himself a snifter of whisky, sat down with the album, and began whiling away the time by flipping through the pictures he'd taken of the girl he'd kept in his basement.

CHAPTER NINETEEN

If he opens the door and he's keeping it together, Eddie told himself, *I won't do it.*

He was standing on Gerry's front stoop, having taken the same path through the snow, he guessed, that the state cop had taken when she'd brought the world crashing down around them. There'd been only one set of tracks, small booted feet that had strode with a purpose to the front door of the most vulnerable pimp in his network.

Eddie rang the bell and knocked, then rubbed his hands together while he waited. Even with gloves on, his fingers felt frozen. The snow and the temperature were both continuing to fall, promising the kind of winter that Maryland hadn't seen in a hundred years. He shivered and rolled his shoulders, trying to dislodge a flake that had somehow found its way down his collar, missing his hair and the coat, and was now melting its way down his back. Maybe a cabin in Maine wasn't what he should be shooting for, after all.

A minute passed and he was getting ready to pound on the door or kick it down when he remembered he was in a suburban neighborhood after midnight. No doubt there was an insomniac neighbor or a nosy old lady just waiting for a minor commotion in the community to break the monotony. One wrong move and he'd be front and center in somebody's binoculars. It was bad enough he'd had to park the Mustang in front of Gerry's house—to put it mildly, a classic muscle car stood out in a suburban neighborhood of family minivans and colorless commuter vehicles. Maybe he should've parked farther away? No, if he needed to get out of there in a hurry, he didn't want to have to sprint through the night to get back to the car.

A shadow moved inside. Eddie cracked his neck, trying to loosen up. He heard a scuffling sound as someone unlocked the security chain, then the dead bolt, then the knob. The door opened.

Gerry stood there, panic written over his face.

"Eddie. Thank Christ you're here," Gerry said, stepping back and motioning him inside. "I'm about to lose my mind, sitting here waiting for the cops."

"Take it easy," Eddie said. He walked through the foyer and into the living room, hands shoved into his jacket pockets, his head on a swivel. He leaned in and poked his head around the corner to check out the dining room and kitchen. "First things first. Did you get the girls out?"

"Yeah. Just like you said. They're all at the Crowne, like it's a normal night."

"They don't know anything?"

"Nope."

"They see the cop when she came around?"

"Trish got a glimpse, but I chased her ass back to her room."

Eddie motioned for the two of them to come into the kitchen, out of sight of the living room windows. Gerry smelled of sweat and aftershave. "Tell me about this state cop."

His pimp started at the top, telling the story in fits and starts, fidgeting with his necklace while he talked, running a fat finger around the gold chain. In the middle of it, he ripped a paper towel off its roll and wiped the sweat off his forehead. For a big guy, he had a high voice.

"So, this Kevin guy was a friend of yours," Eddie said. "He know about me at all?"

"No way," Gerry said, shaking his head from side to side like a bear. "All he knew to do was call the number when he wanted a piece. I took the girl to him."

"He ever go to the Crowne for one of the regular girls?"

Another shake. "He didn't have the nerve. I wanted him and Tiff together to kind of break each other in, you know? Then she could start working the Crowne and maybe he'd be one of our regulars."

"Shitty bad luck that she OD'd with a john who actually knew you," Eddie said. He leaned against the countertop, relaxed, his hands still stuffed in his pockets. His hand accidentally wrapped around his lighter, which made him want a cigarette badly—*very* badly—but that would not be a smart thing to do.

"No kidding," Gerry said, relieved Eddie was seeing this his way. "If it'd been anyone else, all they would have is the phone number."

"So now we have to protect ourselves. The girls are gone, so that's good. I'll move them out of the motel in the next few days so you can lay low. Temporarily, man," Eddie said as Gerry started to protest. "Look, I know you think you can run a string of girls out of your house when the state cops are looking to bust your ass, but why take the chance? You take a call when your phone's tapped or an e-mail when your Internet's being scanned and you're toast. You're going to have to eat this one. We'll let this blow over, then set you up with a new string in a couple of weeks. You'll be making bank before Easter. Okay?"

Gerry nodded, looking at the floor.

"Next, you need to get rid of anything in the house that could incriminate you. If the cops drum up a warrant on some bullshit charge, they could pull you in for something that's not even related to the string. You got anything like that here in the house?"

"Like what?"

"Jesus, Gerry, use your head. Dope. Guns. Money. Anything that would make a cop suspicious."

"Okay, yeah," Gerry said. "There's some stuff."

Eddie raised his eyebrows. "So, get it. We have to clear this place out. Your house has to be like a freaking church."

"What are we going to do with it?"

"There's got to be a twenty-four-hour storage place around here, right?" Eddie asked. Gerry nodded. "Get everything packed. When you're done, I'll take it all over and stow it, then bring you the key. It's a hell of a lot easier to hide a key from the cops than a Glock and a bag of blow, right?"

Gerry looked unsure, but said, "Yeah."

"So get busy," Eddie said, scrubbing his face. "You got any beers around this place?"

"In the fridge," Gerry said, then headed upstairs. "Help yourself."

Eddie grabbed a beer, then stalked the ground level of the house while Gerry banged around on the floor above. He sipped as he checked closets and behind beds, opening drawers and boxes at random. Too much of the girls' junk still lay around. Nothing jumped out right away—there was little personal decoration on the walls, no mementos in the dressers and desks. But there were too many beds in the bedroom. Boxes of condoms. More makeup and clothes than even the average teen used or needed. None of it of the Sunday school variety, either.

There was nothing he could do about it now, of course, but the important thing was that none of it was personalized or identifying. No names, numbers, or pictures. Nothing that could be traced back to him. A mysterious dead end.

Twenty minutes later, Gerry came down the steps carrying two suitcases and breathing hard. He dropped them in the kitchen and looked at Eddie expectantly.

Eddie tipped the bottle back and finished the beer, then gestured at the cases. "That's everything?"

"Everything," Gerry said. "Twenty thou in cash, a baggie of dope, and some blow. And a Glock, believe it or not. You must be psychic."

"You didn't put anything on a computer, did you?"

"Nope."

"Phones? Laptops?"

Gerry reached into his pocket and pulled out his phone. "Just this. And I don't use a laptop. I can barely use the fucking phone."

Eddie turned to put the empty bottle in the sink. "Good. We're going to get through this, bud."

"I sure as hell hope so."

"Grab me a roadie and we'll get out of here."

"Sure, Eddie." Gerry opened the fridge and bent over to grab a beer from the bottom shelf. When he heard the refrigerator door open, Eddie turned away from the sink, pulled out his gun, and—aiming carefully—shot Gerry twice in the back of the head. The shots were deafening claps and the smell pinched Eddie's nose shut. Blood and brains fanned out across the inside of the refrigerator, scarlet against the stark white of the appliance. Gerry's body dropped to the floor, with his chin—the only thing left of his face—coming to rest on the lip of the refrigerator near the vegetable crispers.

Eddie stared at the mess, then carefully put the pistol back in his pocket. A strange odor hung in the air that was more than just the tang of the gunshots, and he breathed through his mouth, telling himself not to think about what he was looking at, what he'd done. Kneeling gingerly beside the body, he fished around Gerry's pocket—his body was still warm—and pulled out his cell phone, which he pocketed. The refrigerator's compressor suddenly kicked on and he jumped like a cat.

Quickly, he grabbed Gerry by the feet and pulled him the rest of the way out of the refrigerator. The chest and head hit the kitchen floor with a wet thump. He closed the refrigerator and the mess with it, then slipped his used beer bottle into a pocket and rinsed the sink.

Careful not to step in the spreading pool of blood, Eddie moved quickly around the first floor cracking open windows, then he shut the heat off at the thermostat and put the air-conditioning on manual. He sprinted up the steps to the second floor to make sure Gerry hadn't been lying about laptops and computers, then grabbed the two suitcases and hurried out of the house, locking the door as he left.

He couldn't do anything to get rid of the tracks, but all the cops would have was his shoe size and the fact he wore one of the most popular brands of boots in the world. He'd touched almost nothing, was taking with him whatever he had, and he was wearing gloves anyway. The suitcases went into the Mustang's trunk. He jumped in the driver's seat and pulled away from the curb, nice and easy. He'd been there thirty-three minutes.

With luck, he'd just severed the most dangerous connection to his past. Now he had to grab Lucy, head north, and capture the future that lay ahead.

CHAPTER TWENTY

She didn't know what to make of Jack. Compared to the man who'd kidnapped her, with the serious expression and strange dead eyes—*Eddie?*—Jack was almost a welcome relief, a living cartoon, capering and cracking bad jokes and dancing in place. He inquired after her health and brought her a hot cup of tea anyway, presenting it with a courtly flourish. She wrapped her hands around it for the warmth, but didn't dare drink it in case it was spiked like the Coke Tuck had given her. It was the first thoughtful gesture anyone had made since her nightmare had begun.

But when he didn't think she was watching, the clownish mask on Jack's face slipped, revealing a weird, disturbing expression. It didn't take a genius to guess what he was thinking, even if he thought he was hiding it behind an act. But she had at least an hour of relative safety—Jack was obviously afraid of Eddie enough to keep his hands to himself. The thought made her shiver. Judging by the way Jack had acted, Eddie's threats were something new and different. Which meant Jack was used to having his way with whoever Eddie normally dropped off.

Maybe that was something she could exploit. *If things are bad,* Chuck had told her once as part of her "training," *and nothing you've done has worked, talk to the guy. Humanize yourself. It's easy for the guy to think of you as an object, a piece of trash. Don't let them do that. Make him see you as a person.*

"Where do you work, Jack?" she asked with a confidence she wasn't close to feeling. He'd made her sit in an easy chair in the corner while he straightened up the living room as though getting ready for a guest.

"Huh?" he said, taken aback. He obviously thought she was mute from fear.

"Where do you work? What do you do for a living?"

"What's it to you?" he asked, squinting at her suspiciously.

"I'm curious what there is to do out here, so far from the city," she said, trying desperately to sound conversational.

"It's not that far," he said defensively. "Twenty minutes to DC, half an hour to Bal'more."

She nodded, encouraging him to talk. "Is there a lot of work around here, then?"

Jack shrugged. "Enough. I pump gas down at the Stop-N-Go on weekends. Mow the grass over at Glenwood Greens when they call."

"Oh? Does that . . . does it pay well?"

He laughed, a sound like a cat scratching at a door. He pulled a rickety dining room chair over and turned it around to sit backwards on it, facing her. "Peasant wages, m'lady. I'm lucky to make enough to eat most weeks."

"Oh," she said, stumped. "I'm sorry."

"No need to be sorry. It's just the way it is," he said, then got an evil look on his face and waggled his eyebrows. "Kind of like the pickle you're in right now."

Lucy swallowed and couldn't stop herself from asking, "Do you know what . . . Eddie is going to do with me?"

"M'lord doesn't confide in the likes of me," he said, back to his courtly demeanor. "I am but a vassal to him, a serf to be used at his convenience."

"What does he . . . usually do with the girls he brings here?"

"Oh, you are far from *usual*. If you were one of Eddie's regular girls, you'd already be at the Fredericksburg rest stop performing fellatio, as the Romans called it, for the truckers. A cute, young thing like you? The semis would be lining up for the chance . . ." Jack's voice trailed off and this time he didn't bother to hide the weird look on his face.

"Are you a collector?" Lucy asked, stumbling over the words as she looked for something to distract Jack. Maybe Eddie's threats weren't going to be enough.

His attention snapped back to the present. "What?"

She gestured around the tiny house. "All of these collectibles. You've got so many . . . things. I guessed you were an antiques collector of some kind."

Jack looked around the room as if the items on the walls had spontaneously sprouted in place. "Oh, I've been buying this stuff for years now. I'm a scholar of the Middle Ages, you might say. The Norman Conquest, Richard the Lionheart, Edward the Black Prince."

"That's so interesting," she said, forcing an element of wonder into her voice.

"I never had the money to go to school for it, but you don't need that to know what you're talking about. Study anything long enough, you can be an expert."

"You're self-taught, then?"

"That's right. Go ahead, ask me something, anything."

Lucy blinked. "Well, what was the Norman Invasion?"

Jack leaned forward, his expression intense. "In the year 1066, France was getting a wee bit crowded. A Frenchman named Willie decided that the isle of Britain was ripe for the picking . . . and he should be the one to pick it. So he gathered an army, one of the largest ever assembled—pikemen and archers and knights and nobles—and sailed across the Channel to challenge the English king, Harold. It was the largest invasion in history to that point. But do you know the most amazing part?"

Lucy shook her head. "No."

"Every single one of his men was named Norman. That's why they called it the Norman Conquest." Jack stared into her face, waiting for a reaction. She looked back at him, at a loss. He leapt to his feet, waving his arms in the air and shouting, "Jesus, Mary, and Joseph, girl. It's a joke. Get it? The *Norman* Conquest?"

Lucy had flinched and cried out when Jack had sprung up, but he hadn't noticed, having already grabbed a plaque off the wall. He gestured at it spastically. The ornament was slightly larger than a dinner plate and made of a thick, dark wood cut in the shape of a shield. Steel rivets outlined the edge. Crossed in the center were a miniature broadsword and mace.

Jack traced the edge of the sword. "Here. See this? See how there's almost no point, but a long edge? Why do you think that was?"

"For chopping?" Lucy said in a small voice.

"No! Well, yes. But that's not why it was the predominant weapon of the period. They couldn't forge the quality of steel needed to keep a point that would do any damage against the armor of the time. So all they did was chop, chop, chop instead of poke, poke, poke."

Jack tossed the plaque behind him without looking and moved to a frame on the wall. It held the floor plan of a castle, poorly drawn in blue ink on lined notebook paper. Arrows and exclamation points pointed to various parts of the schematic.

"And this! Do you know what this is? Huh?"

"No. I'm sorry, I don't," Lucy said, but Jack was too absorbed to hear her.

"This is Château Gaillard, one of the mightiest castles ever constructed. Richard the Lionheart built it in France as a big 'fuck you' to the French king. It held off a siege for over a year and it only fell when one of the king's men climbed through the sewer and right up the shitter. Surprised the hell out of Richard's men. Can you imagine being on the commode and some fella's head pops out of the toilet next to you?"

As Jack droned on about buttresses and parapets, Lucy's eyes dropped from the drawing to the plaque that he'd flung on the table in front of her.

"I made a study of the place, though," Jack continued, stroking his chin. "And I know just where old Richie went wrong. See this curtain wall here? It wasn't crenellated. His men could've held the French off for another six months at least if he would've only spent the money to fortify it properly. Of course, it wouldn't have hurt to put a few bars across the old poop chute, either."

Biting her lip, Lucy inched forward in her seat. Jack was following the line of his drawing with a finger, saying something about barbicans or bartizans. She reached for the edge of the plaque.

Jack turned, looking right at her. "What do you think of my theory?"

Heart pounding, Lucy clasped her hands together and tried to look attentive. "Why . . . um, why didn't he spend the money for the . . ."

"Crenellations," Jack finished for her. He turned back to the wall, shaking his head. "That's a good question. I think it's because he had already taxed the hell out of his peasants and—"

The lecture concluded with a dull *guck* sound as Lucy grabbed the plaque with both hands, stood, then swung it as hard as she could at the back of his head, keeping it flat so that she caught him full-on with the edge. *Like a broadsword*, she thought giddily.

Jack's face slammed into the frame, breaking the glass, and he slid down the wall to fall on the floor. Lucy raised the plaque above her head, breathing heavily and screaming in rage. When Jack didn't move, she lowered the plaque in increments, hardly believing what she'd done. With one toe, she prodded him hard enough to bruise, making sure he wasn't faking. Though it was hard to believe anyone could put on an act after being clobbered like he'd been.

Lucy dropped the plaque with a clatter and staggered into the kitchen. She needed to call for help, to get out of the house, but she was shaking with adrenaline and fear. She clawed at the sink taps and turned on the water so she could gulp directly from the faucet, drinking for long minutes. Finally sated, she splashed her face, then turned to assess her situation.

I need to call Chuck. Eddie or Tuck or someone had taken her phone, but there had to be one in the house. She tore around the dwelling, tipping furniture over, kicking through piles of dirty clothes in the bedroom, and sorting through books about the Middle Ages on the single shelf. There was no sign of a phone.

"You've got to be kidding me," she said out loud. "Who doesn't have a home phone?" *A deadbeat who could barely afford to eat, that's who.*

She started to cry, unable to believe this was happening to her. *Keep it together, Luce,* she could hear Chuck say. *The bad guys win when you give up.* She scrubbed her face with her hands and forced herself to think. If she couldn't call for help, then she'd have to go out and find it.

A closet in the hallway held the basics. Jack's winter jacket smelled like diesel fuel and hot dogs, but it was thick and had a hood. Putting her hands in his grease-stained work gloves was revolting, but the lining was fuzzy and warm. As skinny as he was, a pair of Jack's work pants still easily fit over her own jeans—an extra layer against the cold. She found a flashlight in a dresser drawer. The batteries were nearly dead and the light weak, but it was better than nothing.

After she was outfitted, she went back to the living room, peeking from the doorway to make sure Jack was still unconscious. He hadn't moved. She went to the kitchenette and dug around until she found a filleting knife. That went into a pocket along with a lighter from a kitchen drawer. The food she could find didn't even look edible—the thought of choking down a Vienna sausage from a jar in the refrigerator made her gag, and she didn't want to know what the peanut butter had gone through.

Jack groaned loudly as she closed a cupboard door. A wave of panic flushed through her. She had the knife, but she couldn't bring herself to simply stab him while he was still half-unconscious. She flung open drawers and cupboards at random until she found the ubiquitous junk drawer. *There.* Amid the jumble of loose change and broken pens was a half-used roll of duct tape. Lucy snatched it out of the mess and ran to the living room.

Jack was moving his head slightly and moaning. Moving quickly, she peeled off a three-foot length of tape, pulled his hands behind his back, and wrapped it around his wrists a dozen times. She repeated the maneuver for his feet, using the entire roll, except for a short strip that she slapped over his mouth.

Lucy stood and looked over her handiwork, panting. Jack was trussed like a pig. It wasn't enough to make her feel safe, but it would have to do—time was slipping away. If she didn't get out of the house soon, all of this would be for nothing. Eddie was not the kind to fall for a simple trick, and she wouldn't be able to do anything against him physically. It was time to move.

Taking a deep breath, she opened the door, jumped down the steps, and ran into the night.

CHAPTER TWENTY-ONE

The ringing woke her, but barely.

Three years a cop, two years in the academy, and she still couldn't wake up to a call in the middle of the night. She'd have to work on that.

For now, though, she fumbled for the phone on the side table. When she saw who it was, she swore and remembered why she didn't always respond instantly to a phone call on the wrong side of midnight.

"Jimmy, what do you want?" she said, groaning into the mouthpiece. "It's one in the morning. I got off duty two hours ago."

"Sorry, champ. Thought you might want some news on your, uh, investigation."

Sarah rubbed her eyes. "What investigation?"

"Tiffany? The dead girl hooking for some dude in Glenwood?"

She sat up in bed. *Right, my investigation.* "Yeah, I want to know. What's going on?"

"That guy you paid a visit to? Gerald something?"

"Tena."

"That's him. He's dead."

"*What?*"

"It just came over the wire. I called one of the local Glenwood cops to get the scoop. One of Tena's neighbors was up late walking the dog. They heard two bangs, saw two flashes through Tena's kitchen window, then a car took off a minute later. The neighbor called the police, a cruiser came around, and the officer on the scene found a footprint leading from the front door with a partial outline of blood on it. When he got inside they found Tena."

"The neighbor didn't see the car?"

"Nope, wrong side of the house. But they described the sound of the vehicle as 'deep' and 'powerful.'"

"Shit," she said. "I talked to Tena this afternoon."

"Sounds like you lit a fire," Jimmy said.

"It looks that way. He spooks, calls his boss, and tells him about Tiffany."

"Then the boss decided to cut ties to the pimp who could trace everything back to him."

"Yep." She frowned. "Did the Glenwood cop mention Tena's girls? They weren't in the house, were they?"

"Nope. I didn't ask, but I'm sure he would've mentioned it if, you know, there'd been witnesses or a string of hookers or a couple of extra bodies lying around."

Sarah threw the covers back and swung her feet out of bed. "I've got to get over there."

"Under what pretense? This isn't really your case, you know," Jimmy said. "And I assume you left a trace or two at Tena's house yourself. You nose around this too much and Kline will know you were there."

She pinned the phone to her shoulder with her chin while she shucked off her pj's and grabbed a pair of jeans from the closet. "I'll think of something. But I at least need to ask about the girls. Tena wasn't slick enough to do the recruiting, which means the boss did it for him. They're the only link right now unless the Glenwood cops find a name written in blood."

"Which you wouldn't have access to anyway, since you're not the investigating officer."

"Exactly," Sarah said, hopping around her bedroom on one foot, struggling to slip her socks on. She finally gave in and sat down on her floor with a thump. "The girls are going to disappear. Either the boss has already moved them out or they'll cut and run on their own. There's a very small window to grab one of them and find out what they know."

"Where are you going to look?"

"Are you sitting in front of a computer?"

"Yes," Jimmy said reluctantly.

"Want to do some searching while I get over to the scene?"

"So I'm your support staff now?"

"Hey, chief, you're the reason I'm doing this in the first place," Sarah said. "If it weren't for you, I might be cursing Kline for lifting me off the case, but at least I'd be asleep right now."

"Okay, okay," Jimmy said. "Any thoughts about where he might've stashed the girls? Motel, bus stop, all-night diner?"

Sarah headed for the living room for her coat, then cursed as she stubbed her toe on a chair in the dark. Her apartment was so tiny, the chair was as put away as it could be and she still couldn't avoid smashing a foot into it. "Yeah. Something super temporary and cheap."

"He'd want to keep the girls together, though, so he could pick them up at once. So not too small."

"Good point." Sarah strapped on her gun in a shoulder holster, slipped her badge in a back pocket, then pulled on boots and a thick North Face coat. "Check out the cheap motels in a ten-mile radius. If you don't find anything, move it out five miles and check again."

"Okay."

"Thanks, Jimmy," she said. "I owe you."

"Don't sweat it," he said, dropping his normal mocking tone. "We both knew there was something here and now you know for sure. You rattled somebody when you talked to Tena."

"I just hope it didn't end with him," Sarah said, and ran out of her apartment.

CHAPTER TWENTY-TWO

It was strange driving through the same neighborhood at night, as though she were looking at the photographic negative of a place that she'd taken a picture of during the day—dark where it had been light, crisp silver outlines of roofs and walls and fences that had been indistinct and blurry in the overcast day.

Reflections of flashing red and blue glancing off windows broke the spell as she rounded the last curve. This end of the formerly serene suburb was now lit like a circus. Not only from the police cruisers in front of Tena's home, but from the ambulance and the intense spotlights of a local TV crew. Residual light from the homes in the cul-de-sac illuminated the snow in angular patches as neighbors watched from living room windows, endeavoring to find out what the ruckus was without getting too involved. More adventurous folks were on their front porches and sidewalks in hastily donned combinations of bedroom slippers, sweatpants, and parkas, their breath frosting in the air. A reporter and her cameraman were moving from neighbor to neighbor, interviewing and filming.

Sarah parked four houses down, then walked toward the press of activity cautiously, looking for the officer in charge. The lights in Tena's house were on and the garage door open. A uniformed cop guarded the intersection of Tena's driveway and the street, ready to keep a nonexistent crowd at bay. He was tying off the yellow tape to the street-side mailbox as she approached.

"Can I help you?" he asked as Sarah stopped in front of him. He looked younger than she was.

She plucked her badge from its pocket and showed him. "Maryland State Police. I'd like to speak with the officer in charge."

"Really? You're a statie?"

"Yes, really," she said, peeved. "Hard to believe?"

"Uh, no. I mean, you've got the badge."

"Thanks," she said sourly. "Officer in charge?"

"We didn't get a call from the barracks," he said, frowning. "Is this something official?"

"My interest is personal," Sarah said.

"Personal?" His eyebrows shot to his hairline.

She was glad it was dark as she felt the blood rush to her face. "This homicide may be related to something we're working on, but it's still so thin that we haven't opened a case yet."

The lie sounded ridiculous to her, but the cop nodded amiably. "Okay. Go on in. Jay Saunders is who you want. He's inside, finishing up."

"Thanks."

"Oh," he said as she started for the front door. "You mind using the garage? They want to preserve the tracks by the front door."

"Sure," she said, feeling light-headed. She was out of uniform, of course, and not wearing the boots she'd had on when she'd braced Tena, but that didn't keep her from glancing nervously at the trampled snow leading to the man's front porch. Relief swept through her as she got a good look. It wasn't easy to see in the dark, but instead of crisp, single tracks matching her shoe size, it looked like a herd of elephants had stampeded. *The killer*, she thought, *then the cops on the initial call*. She never thought destruction of evidence and ruining the integrity of a crime scene could make her so happy.

Sarah passed through the garage and into the house through an open side door, clipping her badge to the outside of her coat as she went. The door led to a mudroom; a swinging door was the only exit. Murmuring, maybe three men's voices, came through the door, low and rumbling. Feeling stupid, she knocked, then opened the door to the kitchen.

A strange stink hit her nose. Not the sterile smell of a morgue and not even the rot of cadavers—she'd done her pathology fieldwork. This was more of a bathroom smell combined with an odor of industrial chemicals.

But she forgot the smell as she surveyed the scene in front of her. Sprawled on the floor, with his feet near the sink and its head toward the refrigerator, was the bulky body of Gerald Tena. The fridge door was open—that explained the chemical smell; the refrigerant was pumping into the kitchen—and the inside of it was covered in blood, vibrant against the stark white interior. Congealed bits of flesh had slid down the walls and onto the floor. A carton of orange juice had tipped over in the fridge, spilling its contents on the lowest shelf.

She looked at the body. Aside from two small craters in the back of his head, Tena appeared to be sleeping face-first, but his head was unnaturally flush to the floor and she realized he must be missing most of his face to be lying that way. Heat suffused her face again and her stomach took a strange, sideways lurch. Sarah blinked, striving to keep herself together, but she was sure she was heading for an embarrassing moment when a voice brought her back.

"Don't be sick on my crime scene, now."

She turned her head to look at a middle-aged white man in jeans and a gray Catholic University hoodie, standing in the doorway to the dining room. His face was creased and tired. His expression was one of curiosity, not anger. Behind him were two cops in uniforms, older than the sentry who had been posted outside. Both had what she thought of as the doughnut-shop look: comb-sized mustache, big belly, bright red cheeks. They peered over his shoulder at her.

Sarah took a deep breath. "Detective Saunders?"

"Jay," he said. "Yeah."

"Sarah Haynesworth," she said, motioning toward her badge. "Trooper First Class, out of the Waterloo Barracks."

Saunders nodded but said nothing, just looked at her expectantly.

"I'm working on an . . . issue that might be related to this homicide."

"An . . . issue?" Saunders asked, mimicking the timing of her pause perfectly.

"It's not a case, not yet," she said, hurrying. If she didn't pique Saunders's interest quickly, he'd politely tell her to leave. "But we've had a suspicion that Tena was running a string of girls out of this house. One of those girls suffered an overdose a few days ago. I caught the john trying to bury her in his backyard. The trail led back to Tena, but I've got leads that put him in touch with possibly a much larger network."

Saunders nodded again, then turned to the two uniforms behind him. "Hank, Tommy. Why don't you go through the second floor one more time."

The two looked unhappy, recognizing the dismissal for what it was, but left the dining room without a word. The heavy tread of clomping feet shook the house as they headed upstairs. Saunders fished around in his pockets and brought out a small plastic box.

"Tic Tac?" he offered.

"No, thanks."

He tapped the box until four or five mints spilled onto his palm, then popped all of them into his mouth at once. "Tic Tacs aren't Vicks VapoRub, but they always seem to take the smell away for me."

"Okay, maybe I'll have one," Sarah said.

He shook four into her hand, then put the box away. "So, you've got this issue."

"Yes."

"And we've got a homicide," he said, looking down, almost sadly, at Tena's body.

"Yes, sir."

"First murder case?"

She chewed the inside of her cheek. *Be honest, Sarah.* "Yes."

Saunders nodded, as if confirming something. "I take it you're here fishing for intel."

"Uh . . . something like that," Sarah said.

"But not officially."

"No, sir," she admitted. "Not yet."

"Well, Trooper," Saunders said, putting his hands in his pockets and leaning against the door frame. "Let's get to trading."

CHAPTER TWENTY-THREE

"Well, it definitely fits the stereotype," I said, studying the front of the rather optimistically named Huntington Crowne Motel. At least, that's what I thought the name was. A third of the wooden sign had broken off and dangled facedown on the roof. "It's just missing the village drunk."

As I said it, a gangly man in a dirty T-shirt, with a thick beard and knobby elbows, careened out of the door marked "OFFICE." Slipping on the snow, he wheeled around the corner, skidded to a stop, then bent over, hands on knees and stomach heaving. From where we were parked, he was almost out of sight, but I guessed he wasn't studying patterns of asphalt distribution.

"You're right," Chuck said, shooting me a glance. "That's all it was missing."

I shrugged. The drunk stood unsteadily, wiping his mouth with the back of his hand. He spun in place, raised both middle fingers in the direction of the motel, then stumbled toward a dim future of highway underpasses and park benches.

My attention shifted back to the motel, a sad two-story affair with a flat roof. It was solidly below average in most categories, with a drab gray exterior festooned in meaningless metal rectangles—a cheap architectural decoration that had been popular in the sixties and seventies. Doors to each unit were accessed from the ground floor or via an external catwalk and faced a parking lot of thirty stalls that was half full. Or half empty, I thought, if you were a pimp chasing early retirement and counting every customer.

The traffic we'd seen going in and out of the lot made it a safe bet that we'd found the place Tuck had described. In ten minutes I'd already watched two guys, both walking with an odd hitch in their step—construction workers or truckers, by the look—come out of different rooms, then get in their cars and leave. No sooner had their headlights faded than a small SUV pulled into the lot and a skinny guy in a cheap-looking suit unwittingly took the spot of the first john, then went to the door of yet a third unit and knocked. Dull yellow light beamed from inside as the door was opened and a price negotiated. The man went inside, then the light winked out.

"What's our play?" I asked. I fished a tissue from a pocket and wiped my constantly running nose.

"We could go door to door. Roust the johns until we find Lucy."

"Subtle," I said. "And not without its charm. I've always wanted to see a motel full of half-naked dudes holding their Johnsons and running for their cars at top speed."

"Don't forget the girls spitting on us for trashing their quota for the night."

"Oh, right. I forgot that part," I said. "Do you have a plan B?"

Chuck rubbed the silver ball-and-post piercing that went through his right eyebrow. "No way this place can run without the managers knowing. And getting a cut. So we go in, brace the night manager, say we're looking for one girl in particular, and that's it. We ain't here to rock the boat, we don't want to shut him down. We want one girl and one girl only. If he cooperates, everything keeps running smoothly."

"Offer the carrot first, huh?" I said. "What if he doesn't cooperate?"

"I'll pull his ears off and switch them."

"The stick, I take it."

"Yep," he said. We looked up as the guy in the cheap suit came out of the room and strode to his car, hands jammed deep in his pockets. I pulled my sleeve back to glance at my watch and Chuck snorted. Headlights came on, illuminating the side of the motel, then the SUV left quickly, spinning its tires on the ice that had gathered in the dip where the lot met the road. The engine's sound faded into the distance. We sat in the dark.

"You thinking of something?" Chuck asked.

I cleared my throat. "What happens to the rest of these girls once we find Lucy?"

He was quiet for a moment. "I'm not out to save the world, Singer. Not tonight. I get Lucy home safe, I'll put my cape back on, sure. But later. Right now, I just want to find my sister."

I couldn't argue with that. "Let's do it, then."

Chuck started the car and pulled into the lot. Ignoring the open parking stalls, he cruised straight to the office door and shut off the car. We got out and simultaneously cinched our belts and adjusted our coats as we walked to the door, surreptitiously checking our sidearms. If the manager happened to like the cut he was getting, and thought we were there to end the gravy train, he might take exception and decide it was worth ventilating the two of us to keep the status quo.

I followed Chuck inside. An entry bell tinkled as we came through the door. The office was numbingly mediocre. Marbled gray-green linoleum covered the floor, while the walls were painted in thick swatches of peach. Vinyl chairs that had looked dated in the eighties sat in opposite corners of the room. Perched on a stool behind the counter was a thirty-something reading a copy of *Computer Gaming Planet*. Poker-straight brown hair fell past his ears, like a bowl cut let go six months too long. A mustache enhanced, rather than diminished, a catastrophic overbite. Glasses with thick black rims completed the picture of a guy who could only get a job as the night manager of a hooker's motel. A nameplate on a tripod informed us that this was Paul.

His head stayed bent as we approached the counter. "I don't handle transactions," he said in a bored voice. "Talk directly to the girls, man."

Chuck reached across and plucked the magazine from the guy's hands, who gave a halfhearted "Hey." Chuck held the magazine at arm's length, ripped it in half, in half again, then tossed the pieces onto the counter. "I'm here to talk to you, asshole."

Paul's jaw dropped, then his hands moved lower behind the counter. In one smooth motion, I drew my SIG from its holster, pointed it at his nose, and said, "Reach for the sky." There was a slight pause, then the guy's hands floated past his ears until they were straight up and down like toothpicks.

"We got your attention?" Chuck asked.

"Dude, what do you want?" His eyes were enormous, watching the end of my gun like it was the gateway to another dimension.

"We want to talk."

"About what?"

For safety's sake, I went around the counter and gently pushed the Employee of the Month off the stool and out of the way, then looked under the counter. Expecting a shotgun or a cheap street pistol, I was thrown when all I found were a few old *Playboy*s and an aerosol can of what I thought was pepper spray. Frowning, I grabbed the can, then held it up for Chuck to see.

"Fuck is that?" he asked.

"Deodorant," I said. "He was going to Right Guard us to death."

I put my gun away, then—on a whim—sprayed Paul on the arm. He yelped and kind of jumped in place, like I'd stuck him with a knitting needle. I looked at Chuck. "This is going to be the easiest interrogation in the history of law enforcement."

Paul's eyes bugged out even farther. "You guys are cops? Oh, God. Oh, Jesus."

Chuck pulled out his badge and gave Paul a minute to study it. "Arlington PD. And, before you ask, yeah, I'm outside of my jurisdiction. And, no, that don't matter. Do you know why?"

Paul shook his head.

"Because you're an accessory to so many misdemeanors and felonies that there ain't a judge in the world who would care if I came from Virginia or South Dakota or the Congo. But that's not the important part."

"It's not?"

"No. The important thing is," Chuck said, leaning in, "I'm not here to bust you."

"You're not?"

"No, Paul. All I want to know is if there's one girl here. Just one. Tell me the truth and I'll walk out of here."

"O-okay," he stuttered. "Which girl?"

My mouth went dry. We'd loosened up a little, had some fun. Now the rubber was hitting the road.

"Her name is Lucy. Asian girl. Sixteen. Slim, long black hair, about five seven." When Paul looked doubtful, Chuck said, "Not a regular. She would've been brought here earlier tonight, a couple of hours ago at the most."

Paul shook his head. "Sorry, man."

"Come on. You know every girl that works here, just like that?"

"No, but there's never been an Asian. All the girls are just regular, you know, white trash from Baltimore and Bowie. Nothing, uh, special."

Chuck got an ugly look on his face and, almost faster than I could follow, he came halfway across the counter and slapped Paul across the side of the head, sending his glasses flying.

"Whoa, whoa, whoa," I said, holding Paul upright with one hand and shoving Chuck away with the other. "Jesus, Chuck. Cool it. We need him to talk."

Paul held the side of his face, where a livid red mark showed where Chuck had connected. "Holy crap," he said once, then kept whispering it. Spit dribbled out of one side of his mouth. "What is wrong with you, man? I told you, we don't have any Asian chicks here. We just don't."

"You got ten seconds to tell me who brings the girls here," Chuck said. "I want a name, the car he drives, what time he shows or I swear to God I will shoot you in the head."

By the look on Chuck's face, this might not be an act. I was wondering exactly what I was going to do if he decided to make good on the threat when the decision was taken out of my hands. The little bell on the door tinkled and a petite black girl came through the door, dressed in jeans and a massive winter coat.

But what really grabbed my attention was the chunky Glock 22 she was pointing at us.

CHAPTER TWENTY-FOUR

"Is this thing coming apart?"

"*No,*" Eddie said forcefully, struggling for control. He closed his eyes briefly and softened his voice. "No. Everything is on track."

"You took care of your little problem?"

"Yes. We're in good shape. The detour took less time than I thought." There was a long pause on the other end and Eddie wondered if Torbett was going to back out. His throat constricted at the thought. "Look, this isn't easy. There are a lot of moving parts and making it work on the fly is going to mean there'll be a couple of bumps along the way. But that's all they are, bumps. You hired me to do the job and it will get done. It's *getting* done."

"I can't afford any mistakes, Eddie. If you draw attention to yourself and I'm caught anywhere near you, it'll ruin me."

"You won't suffer any damage on this, I swear," Eddie said, struggling to project confidence and not desperation. "Believe me, I've got my own reasons for making sure the deal goes off without a hitch."

Another pause. Then, "Convince me."

Eddie closed his eyes again. You couldn't snow people all the time. Sometimes the best, most reliable method to get someone on your side was to surprise them with the truth. Or half of it. "I've got something that depends on this deal. Something . . . big in my life. Not another score, something personal. And if I don't get your money, that something is going away. And I don't know if I can live with that."

Silence.

Eddie swallowed. "That's why I'm going to make sure I get this girl to you. This isn't just a deal to me. It's everything."

The lights of the highway flew by as the silence stretched on. The Mustang gurgled and clacked beneath him as Eddie strained to hear. He wondered if he'd said too much, if his confession could be used against him or had turned Torbett off somehow. What the man on the other end of the line said next would mark his future. Miles seemed to tick away as he waited for an answer.

"All right."

Eddie let out a breath and his shoulders slumped in relief. "Then we're good? Stick to the plan?"

"Yes."

"Okay," Eddie said, eager to be off the phone now. "Anything else?"

Torbett hesitated, making a weird sighing noise Eddie had heard only once before, when he'd delivered the last girl and, as brusque and businesslike as he'd been only a moment ago, he was just as suddenly stuttering and unsure. "Could you . . . could you put her on the phone? Just for a minute."

Eddie glanced over at the empty seat. "Ah, sorry. She's been out cold for the last hour. I had to dope her to keep her from screaming her head off."

"You didn't hurt her, did you?" Torbett asked, his voice veering from dreamy to sharp. "You can forget it if she's been bruised or manhandled."

"That's why I drugged her."

"I don't want a junkie, either."

Eddie took a deep breath. "They were just roofies. Her body will flush them in about six hours. And the guy I got her from told me she's completely straight otherwise. Doesn't drink, doesn't smoke, doesn't do drugs. Clean as a whistle."

Torbett sighed. Another long pause. Another sigh. Eddie's panic bobbed to the surface again. Torbett's little noises sounded like the preamble to *No* all over again. "Look, I—"

"Do you want a picture?" Eddie said, interrupting. "She's right here."

Silence. Then, "Yes."

"Hold on." Eddie fumbled with his phone as he flew along the road, raking through his stored pictures without slamming the car into a telephone pole. With a few taps, he sent the picture of Lucy from earlier in the night to Torbett's cell number. "On its way."

He squeezed the phone until a throaty sigh made its way through from the other end. "She's beautiful."

"She is," Eddie said. "And she'll be yours by the end of the night."

Yet another pause. This was it. Eddie's heart drummed in his chest as he waited for the answer.

"I'll see you there," Torbett said and hung up.

Eddie ended the call, his shoulders slumping in relief, while sweat prickled his scalp and beaded his forehead. His fish had jumped back on the hook, but barely. The thought of losing his bankroll made Eddie nauseous. Everything depended on having a buyer and not just because he needed the money—with Gerry on his rap sheet now, he couldn't afford to have the guy with the money back out of the deal. There was no going back and, without cash, no going forward, either.

He rolled the windows down, hoping the blast of frozen air would quell his nerves, which were thrumming like an electric current. He scrubbed his face, willing himself to focus. Until the call from Torbett, he'd been able to tuck away thoughts of Gerry into a dim corner of his mind to deal with later. But now all he could see was the scarlet spray against the white walls of the refrigerator.

He'd never killed anyone before. Beat the shit out of a couple girls, gotten into some terrific fights, sure. He'd seen violence and had been on the receiving end a few times. Like the time he'd been knifed and hit the guy with a cue stick so hard he thought, yeah, maybe he'd killed him. He heard later that the sucker had recovered. Couldn't count to twenty, but he was alive.

This thing with Gerry was different. So different. He hadn't killed him in a bar fight while he was crazy drunk or screaming mad. He'd simply . . . killed him. Maybe worse, he'd acted like he was helping him, had promised to make things right. He'd made a conscious, cold-blooded decision to end the guy's life, just in case.

In case the cop came back around. *In case* Gerry talked. *In case* a loose end tied him to Gerry. He'd shot someone twice in the head as a precaution.

The sweat was frozen on his head and his teeth began to chatter, but Eddie kept the windows down, driving faster. He was going to face this. How did it feel to end someone on the off chance something might go wrong? What did it mean to go down this path, no matter how good his reasons were?

He examined his thoughts and feelings, attempting to analyze himself dispassionately. Long minutes passed, then he gave up and rolled up the windows to concentrate on the road, unsure if it should scare him that he didn't feel guilty . . . or that he didn't feel anything at all.

CHAPTER TWENTY-FIVE

"Hands on the back of your head. Now."

The look on Chuck's face said, *You've got to be kidding*, but he put his hands parallel to his ears anyway. I wove my fingers together and cupped the back of my head, watching the girl. At first I thought that she was, I don't know, in high school—she didn't look more than eighteen—but she had us covered like a pro, holding a Weaver stance like she'd been born to it.

To my right, and for the second time tonight, Paul raised his hands like he was trying to tickle the ceiling. Out of the side of my mouth, I said, "This has been one lousy shift for you."

"Sir, no talking," the girl barked. "Come around the counter. One at a time."

I did what she said. Paul followed. I could smell his nervous sweat. The foyer was now uncomfortably crowded with three adult men and a girl armed with a howitzer and a decidedly unfriendly expression on her face. Chuck, who'd had his back turned to the door, still didn't know who or what was behind him. For that matter, neither did I, but I could take an educated guess.

"She's on our team," I said when Chuck caught my eye. "Only a cop calls someone 'sir' in a situation like this."

Keeping his hands in the air, Chuck tilted his head back and said to the ceiling, "Officer, I'm Detective Chuck Rhee, Arlington PD Gangs Unit. My lieutenant's name is John Creusfeld. My colleague here is Marty Singer, formerly of DC Homicide."

"It's Trooper, not Officer," she said. "Who's your other friend?"

"This is Paul," I said. "And he chose the wrong occupation after high school."

"Sir, he can answer for himself," the girl said.

"I'm Paul, the night manager," he said. "And he's right. I wish I was stocking shelves right now."

There was a pause. "I really am a cop," Chuck said. "You can call my lieutenant if you want."

"Badge?"

"Yes."

"Where? Tell me, don't show me."

"Back left pants pocket," Chuck said.

"Take it out with your right hand," she said. "Not your left."

Neat trick, I thought, as I watched Chuck, as flexible and lanky as anyone I knew, contort his body to comply. If he had anything dangerous in his back pocket, she'd see it coming from a mile away. He finally fished the badge holder out of his pocket.

"Show me. Next to your head," she instructed. He did so and the cover fell open, revealing the gold-and-blue shield of Arlington County. "Hand it back."

Chuck extended his arm behind him as far as he could and she took the badge from him. She held it eye-high so she could watch us as she studied it. I watched as her expression changed three or four times, making it clear that we were one of the last things she'd expected to find here. She'd have to work on her game face if she didn't want every scumbag she nabbed reading her like a book.

"Are you armed?" she asked.

"I have my service weapon," Chuck said. "Marty's carrying."

"Licensed," I said before she shot me.

Her eyes flicked over to Paul. "What about you?"

He shook his head, but I said, "Right Guard."

"What?"

"They were all out of Secret," I said. "Strong enough for a man, though."

Her face tightened. *We are not amused.* I shrugged. It probably wasn't the best time for humor, but Chuck was ready to blow a gasket if the cadet here didn't let us get back to finding Lucy.

But she seemed just as ready to get to the point. She eased out of her stance, although the gun stayed ready at her side. "Does Arlington PD always beat their interrogation subjects, Detective?"

"I'm not that kind of cop," Chuck said. "But I needed intel and I can't wait."

"Is that going to help explain what you're doing in Maryland?"

"Do you mind if we put our hands down now?" I asked. It was embarrassing, but my shoulders actually ached.

"Go ahead," she said. "Keep them in sight."

Chuck lowered his hands with care and slowly turned in place. The girl handed him his badge back. "You mind telling us who you are?"

"Sarah Haynesworth," she said, pulling her own badge and holding it so we could see. "Maryland State Police."

"What are you doing here?" I asked.

"You first," she said, then surprised me with a smile. "I'm the arresting officer, after all."

Chuck filled her in on our night, from the first stirring of fear he'd had when Lucy hadn't called for their dinner date to the point just before she'd walked in on us. Halfway through the explanation, she holstered her gun and leaned against the wall.

"So," Chuck finished, "this fleabag motel is all we got. One thread, leading back to the son of a bitch who took my sister."

I cleared my throat. "Now maybe you can understand why Chuck was using, uh, advanced interrogation techniques."

"That's our story," Chuck said. "And, no offense, but we need to get back to it."

"What's your plan?" Sarah asked.

"I need to find the pimp who's running the girls here. Find him and either he'll still have her or know where she's at. This fool," Chuck said, pointing to Paul with his chin, "probably don't know much, but he's got to know who's in charge of the girls."

"Who will be the guy your sister's boyfriend told you about?"

"Yeah," Chuck said, then turned to Paul. "How about it, champ? You know who runs the show?"

Paul shook his head timidly. "I don't, man. I just sit at the desk . . ."

Chuck swore and Paul cringed, as if expecting to get hit again. I kept my face blank, but my heart sank. If this was a dead end—or Tuck had simply lied—then this was it. The best we could do is file a missing persons report, wait for the Amber Alert, and hope someone at a rest stop or gas station spotted Lucy.

"Do you know Gerry?" Sarah asked. "Big, sloppy guy with a mustache and gold chain?"

"Gerry?" Paul said, surprised. "Yeah, he's the one who drops the girls off."

"Who's Gerry?" Chuck and I asked at the same time.

"I didn't get to tell you what I'm here for," Sarah said.

"Now's the perfect time," I said.

"I've been tracing a network of hookers and low-level pimps stretching west of Baltimore and north of DC. They're all tiny operations, sometimes as few as one guy and two girls. But the pimps have never done the recruiting. They're more like . . . managers."

"That's this guy Gerry?" Chuck asked.

She nodded. "I got his ID yesterday from a john who'd . . . used one of his girls. She'd overdosed while she was with him. When he thought we were going to pin a murder rap on him, he coughed up Gerry's name. I traced him to his house and paid him a visit, which I think shook him, but I didn't have anything else, so I had to go."

"But the question is," I said, "if Gerry's only a manager, who's supplying the girls?"

"Right. I've been picking up signs that it's just one smooth talker who's been convincing local girls into hooking. He doesn't strong-arm them—he brainwashes them into thinking they're in love or this is a better life than they're leaving at home."

I glanced at Chuck. "Our man."

Sarah nodded again. "I didn't have a name, but it makes sense. Whoever this CEO is, he let Gerry run his string of girls out of this place, so Paul never met the guy."

"We got to get to this guy Gerry. It's the link we were looking for . . ." Chuck said, then trailed off as Sarah shook her head. "What?"

"Gerry took two bullets in the back of the head sometime in the last four hours. I just came from the crime scene."

I swore. "He's covering his tracks."

"Anything at the scene?" Chuck asked, a thin note of desperation in his voice.

"That's how I knew to come here," she said, her face sympathetic. "A pack of matches and a little legwork from a friend. And it's the seediest motel in the area. But I'm not sure there was anything else, Rhee. I'm sorry. I can put you in touch with the detective who's in charge of the homicide."

Chuck's shoulders slumped.

I said, "What about the girls? They might know something."

"Runaways, Singer," Chuck said. "They're not going to know shit."

"They might," I said cautiously. I didn't want to get his hopes up, but I wasn't ready to throw in the towel, either. "We've talked about how what he's doing with Lucy doesn't fit the MO. It's a regular kidnapping, not a bait-and-switch to get her to sell herself willingly."

Sarah shrugged, nodded. Chuck stared at the floor.

"And, killing this guy Gerry," I continued, exploring the idea. "It smells desperate. Pimps aren't hit men. The ones in the city aren't anyone to mess with, but some amateur out in the boonies—even an entrepreneurial one—isn't going to go around snuffing people at the drop of a hat."

"What's your point, Singer?"

"I think," I said, choosing my words carefully, articulating the idea even as I was saying it, "that this isn't business as usual. It's a big play."

"What do you mean?" Sarah asked.

"I think he's selling her," I said. "And for so much money, he's willing to start shooting people to protect the deal. Maybe that wasn't the original plan. Maybe he meant to make his money *and* keep running the girls."

"But then I braced his pimp," Sarah said. "He caught wind of it and that was the end of Gerry. The boss started cutting ties on his one-way ticket out of town."

"You think the girls might know what this big deal is?" Chuck asked me.

I shrugged. "If they hated his guts, probably not. But some might be more or less in love with him. Maybe they talked about their hopes and dreams. Maybe he let slip that he had a big payday on the horizon . . . and where it was coming from."

We were quiet for a minute.

"Let's go," Chuck said, then gave voice to what we were all thinking, but were too afraid to say. "It's all we got."

CHAPTER TWENTY-SIX

How long could a road be?

The lights of Jack's home had long since faded into the darkness and Lucy already felt like she'd been walking all night. Heat had been leaching from her body from the moment she'd stepped off the porch and the blackness of the night was so absolute, she felt as if she were wearing a hood over her head. The combined elements made it feel as if she was walking on a treadmill in the dark. She could be walking in circles or down a dead end, for all she knew. Maybe she was still unconscious and this was the worst of all nightmares. Or she was already dead and this was all there was. Her mind began to flirt with the edge of panic as she considered the possibility that life after death was to walk forever in the dark and the cold.

Stop it. Two things told her she wasn't imagining it all: the edge of the pavement by her feet and the thin cone of light emanating from the flashlight in her hand. Without the light, in fact, she was sure she would've gone crazy in the first ten minutes, if she wasn't already. She would've simply . . . given up. But with Jack behind her and woods to either side, there was nowhere to go except forward. The easiest thing to do—the best thing to do—was to force herself to focus on the simple mechanics of putting one foot in front of the other. *All roads lead somewhere, right?*

Unfortunately, while the monotony of clomping alongside the road helped her calm down, it also let her mind wander.

It was crazy how dependent she was. Without a watch, she didn't know the time. Without a phone, she couldn't call for help. Without the flashlight in her hand, she would've crawled into a hole and died. With a cop for a brother, and living so close, she'd let herself just ignore the dangers that probably every other girl her age thought about all the time.

Some guy won't leave you alone? Call Chuck. Stranded downtown and it's too late to catch the Metro? Call Chuck. If she got out of this mess, she promised herself, she wouldn't take him or her *jobumo* for granted, no matter how much they both got on her nerves sometimes. And she'd also pay more attention to how dangerous and unpredictable life could be.

Like who she dated. Tuck, that creep. That was another promise she could make. If he thought she'd kicked his ass before—when he'd grabbed her and tried to pin her down, telling her it was time for her to give "it" to him—he was going to get the surprise of his life. Just imagining her foot being planted against the side of his head in a perfect circle kick gave her energy. Which she needed, since her teeth were literally chattering from the cold.

But then thoughts of Tuck put her situation squarely back in front of her. As in, who was this guy Eddie and what had he planned to do with her? It hadn't taken long to figure out that he hadn't wanted to rape her or even hurt her—it made her queasy to think about, but if that had been the goal, it would've happened before she'd even come to in

The Wicked Flee

his car. Not that he had her best interests at heart, that was for freaking sure, but what did he want with her then?

When do you handle something you don't care about . . . with care?

She went cold inside when the answer, so obvious, stared back at her.

When it was a delivery.

She wasn't a person to Eddie, she was a package. An object that had been requested, paid for, and was on its way to be delivered. And delivered intact. It all made a sick kind of sense. Eddie refusing to hit her, offering her water and a coat, threatening Jack if he so much as touched her.

The thought made her sick all over again, followed by a thought that astounded her, a revelation—someone had *ordered* her, like a hamburger or a book or a movie. She was an object to someone out there who didn't know a thing about her or care if they did. And whoever that was, *they* were the one who wanted her for sex or worse. It could be the only reason Eddie hadn't touched her and warned Jack not to, either.

The thought was horrifying, frightening, enraging. Her feet were numb from the cold, but she stamped them on the ground with twice the force than she needed to out of anger. A minute ago, only Tuck had been in her sights. Now she had a list. It started with Tuck, went through Eddie, and ended with whoever had made the mistake of adding her to their wish list.

With her head bent against the wind and her eyes locked on the little splash of illumination from her flashlight, Lucy was so focused that she didn't see the headlights until they were close enough to blind her. For an instant, instinct urged her to turn and bolt into the woods. But she stopped herself. This was what she'd been looking for, a car or a person or a business where she could get some help, call the police, or at least hide from Eddie. Unless it *was* Eddie.

She relaxed as the car, a red Ford Focus, stopped next to her. A woman—white, maybe fifty, with fake, brassy blonde hair—looked at her in surprise and concern from behind the wheel. A thick white scarf hid the lower half of her face, while a bulky Ravens team coat seemed to swallow her body. The driver's window was down and heat emanated in delicious waves from inside the vehicle. Lucy was so cold, her body automatically gravitated a step closer to the car.

The woman pulled the scarf down past her mouth. "Honey, are you all right? What are you doing out on the road at this time of night?"

"Please," Lucy said. Her chin and lips were so cold they felt like rubber, making it hard to talk. "I need help. I just—I know it sounds crazy—but I just escaped from some lunatic at the end of the road. He was keeping me for this other man who kidnapped me last night. I need to call my brother. I need to get out of here."

"Oh my God," the woman said, her mouth and eyes describing the same *O* of surprise. "Of course I can help, honey. Get in. There's a police station half an hour from here. One of the cops there is a friend of mine."

Lucy moved around the car as fast as she could and slid into the passenger's seat. Once she was inside, the smell of beer and perfume made her wince, but the heat felt so good that the car could've smelled like anything and she still would've been happy. She held her hands against the vents. Her arms were shaking and her muscles twitched.

"Thank you," she said, her voice breaking. "Thank you so much."

The woman executed a three-point turn in the middle of the road, then took off the way she'd come. "Is that warm enough for you?"

"It's wonderful," Lucy said, her head spinning at how her luck had turned around. An hour ago, she'd been kidnapped and on her way to become some faceless sex maniac's toy. Now she might be an hour from being back home.

"You were kidnapped?" the woman asked. "And you were being held somewhere? How in the world did you escape?"

Lucy described the night from the beginning at Tuck's until the moment she'd seen the woman's car. The woman oohed and aahed at every sentence, interjecting with "Get out of town!" and "Oh my God!" several times.

"You know what?" the woman asked rhetorically when Lucy had finished. "I should call my friend right now and tell him about this. He might want to haul out to this guy Jack's house and collar the creep right now."

She fished around in a side pocket of the Ravens jacket and pulled out a cell phone with a scarlet, sequined cover. With practiced ease, she glanced down at the phone once and found the number she wanted from her speed dial list. Lucy could hear the phone ringing. A voice answered.

"Hey, it's me," the woman said. "I just found a cute little Asian girl wandering along Platter's Lane, frozen to the bone and scared to death. Said she was kidnapped last night, got taken to some man's house, and barely escaped with her life."

The voice said something on the other end.

"Uh-huh," the lady replied. "She said that she—what's your name, hon?"

"Lucy."

"Lucy? Okay—Lucy said that she clobbered the guy, then headed for the road on foot, hoping to find help. I know, can you believe it?"

The voice said more in a quizzical tone.

"What? No, I don't think so." The woman pulled the phone away and turned to Lucy. "He wants to know if the man, you know, touched you. Should we be going to the hospital instead?"

"Oh, no. He didn't do anything like that," Lucy said. "He looked like he wanted to, but we never got that far. I guess I knocked him out before he could try anything."

The woman put her phone back to her ear. "She says no, she blasted him before he could try. What? Yeah, that probably makes sense. Where?"

Murmuring on the other end.

"Okay, I'll see you there," the woman said and, glancing briefly at the screen, hung up and slipped the phone back in her pocket. She looked over at Lucy. "He says he's actually just around the corner. We'll meet him, then he can take you back to the station to help you."

"May I use your phone?" Lucy said. "My brother is a cop, too. I know he's out looking for me and I'd like to let him know I'm okay."

The woman's face wrinkled apologetically. "Oh, honey. I'm sorry, my battery's almost out and my husband's going to be worried if he doesn't hear from me soon. My police friend is only five minutes away. Can you wait that long?"

"I guess so," Lucy said in a small voice, then sank back into the seat. She gazed out the window as they drove, watching blindly as the night passed by. Now that the fear and terror were gone, the adrenaline was going, too, leaving her feeling hazy and not quite fully awake as the warmth crept through her body. *It's so remote out here*, she thought. *I feel like I haven't seen a light in hours.*

The woman made lefts and rights down fence-lined country roads, humming to herself, glancing occasionally at Lucy and smiling. She took a left at a lonely four-way stop. A convenience store, brightly lit in white-and-yellow lights, seemed to sprout out of the ground at the corner. The woman pulled into a parking slot in front of the store and put the car in park. She took out her phone, poked at a few buttons, then lifted it to her ear again.

"I'm here," she said after a moment, then twisted in her seat to look behind them. "Yeah, I see your lights. See you in a minute."

She put the phone away and smiled at Lucy. "Almost here."

Lucy struggled to sit up, fumbling with the seat belt. As she got the buckle undone, she heard the deep, throaty growl of a powerful engine as a car came to a bucking stop in the parking spot next to her.

She barely had time to turn in her seat before the door opened and a face bent down to look at her. When she saw who it was, she opened her mouth to scream, but the woman behind her reached forward and covered Lucy's mouth with her scarf like it was a garrote.

"Hello, Lucy," Eddie said. The lump on his forehead pulsed angrily and the look on his face was unsmiling and steely. "It's good to see you again."

CHAPTER TWENTY-SEVEN

"Daddy?" Sarah said, holding the phone up and looking at the hooker skeptically. "Seriously?"

The girl sitting on the edge of the bed shrugged and turned her head to stare into the corner of the room. She was thin and tall, with a long neck accentuated by a white tank top and dark black hair gathered in a bun. Skinny legs sprouted from cutoff jeans, the outside seams of which were cut extra short to expose as much thigh as possible. Footwear was a pair of yellow flip-flops despite the subzero temperatures outside. Her face, though thin, was made up of soft lines. Sarah would eat her hat if the girl was seventeen.

Playing the only lead they had, the three of them had decided to split up, with Rhee going solo while Singer stayed with her. She didn't appreciate the sidekick, but Singer had pointed out that his involvement in whatever it was they were doing wasn't even remotely official and it would be nice if he had some cover from the only ranking Maryland cop among them. Chuck was out of his jurisdiction, but at least he had a badge.

Sarah hadn't liked the reasoning. The likelihood of the local police arriving on the scene was slim to none. Who was going to call them? The girls wouldn't dare, their pimp was dead, and the local PD was either being paid to ignore the motel or they considered it such a low priority that it amounted to the same thing. Cops making a random check on the Crowne? Not gonna happen.

Which was all to the good, since she was so far from being aboveboard on this that Kline wouldn't have to file a report to fire her ass, he'd simply laugh her off the force. And, from Rhee's description of their reasons for being here, he and Singer had gone off the rails the minute they'd started looking for Rhee's sister.

But she knew competence and motivation when she saw it and these two had it in buckets. They moved like partners and, despite their reasons for being there, had exuded calm—even when she'd pointed her Glock at them. Even when they all knew they belonged to the same club, neither one had tried to pull rank on her or feed her a line of bull.

True, she hadn't liked what she'd seen from Rhee, when he'd knocked the manager around, but after learning what he was after, she understood the situation better. If her sister were still alive and Sarah could've saved her by slapping someone in the head, Paul would've lost more than his glasses. In any case, it would be nice to have backup on this little mission of hers, even if they did amount to the law enforcement version of the Keystone Kops.

So, with Singer in tow and her badge at the ready, Sarah had started banging on doors. Most had opened to reveal nervous junkies or weary immigrant workers stuffed six to a room. A girl had answered their knock on the fifth door. The look on her face was simultaneously bored and faux coquettish, an expression that changed rapidly to fear and dismay when she saw the badge. She'd made a halfhearted attempt to shut the door on them, but Singer had planted his foot in the frame, allowing Sarah to bull her way in.

While she talked to the girl, Singer searched the room, revealing no coat, no shoes except the flip-flops, no purse or wallet or keys. But what Trish, the girl, was lacking in basic human needs she made up for in tools of the trade. A twenty-four box of condoms, a makeup bag, and a cheap, disposable cell phone. The phone had contained just one number in its contact list and call history: *Daddy*.

"Trish, do you remember me? I was the one who came to the house yesterday," Sarah said. "You peeked out from around the corner."

The girl nodded. "I remember."

"What are you doing here, Trish?"

"Nothing."

Sarah crossed her arms. "If I asked the motel manager how often you're here, what do you think he'd say?"

A shrug.

"You have any family in the area? Somebody I can call?"

"No." Softly.

"You want to tell me about all these texts, Trish?" Sarah asked.

She shook her head.

"Nothing? You won't mind if I send a couple, then?"

A shrug.

"Should I call Daddy and see what he says?"

Trish opened her mouth, fear flashing across her face, then her shoulders slumped, resignation taking its place. Singer saw it, too, and caught Sarah's eye. He made a gesture with his fingers. *Let's switch.*

Sarah bristled. She couldn't get through to a teenage black girl, but the middle-aged white guy would? Singer waited, watching her with those calm green eyes, letting her come to the conclusion he knew she would. *Do you want to make some headway on this thing or do you want to play ego games?*

She swallowed her pride and went to search the bathroom again, more to give him some room to operate than to look for clues. What she really wanted to do, despite the fact that it was hella-freezing, was step outside to get some air, to get away from the room and everything it represented. And not because it smelled like sex. It did, but that wasn't what was causing a crawling sensation under her skin. The odor was repugnant but understandable. She struggled to put a name to what her senses were telling her, then she had it.

The room smelled like people.

The tiny space had all the combined odors of a subway car or a taxicab or a crowd pressed to the edge of a concert stage. It was sweat and heat and moisture and all the smells that the human body makes when it's moving, working, rutting. To that cocktail, her fertile imagination added the despair of the girls and the vulgarity of the act done for commerce and greed. The impact of what Trish did and went through dozens of times a day hit Sarah like a physical thing. Pulling her shirt over her nose, she took a deep breath, sick and dizzy, trying to clear her head.

She backed out of the bathroom like it was a crime scene and turned around to see how Singer was doing. He'd dragged the room's single chair close to Trish, directly in front of her, but careful to stay out an arm's length away. At first Sarah thought this was excessive caution on his part—how dangerous did he think the girl was?—then she realized he'd done it for Trish, not him. She took a second, careful look at how he was sitting. His posture was relaxed, his elbows on the arms of the chair and his hands clasped together. Head canted forward, interested. Expression concerned but laid-back, with the intensity dialed down. Sarah leaned against the bathroom door frame, the revulsion of a second ago forgotten in her curiosity.

Singer's deep voice murmured occasionally, but he'd gotten Trish to talk and was letting her go, encouraging her with a nod or a gesture when she slowed. They stayed that way for several long minutes.

Singer's presence seemed comforting enough to put her at a cautious ease. Eventually, the dialogue wound down and Singer glanced at Sarah. She walked over.

"Trish, Officer Haynesworth and I are going to step outside for a second," Singer said to the girl.

"Can I have my phone back?" she asked.

"In one second," he said, opening the door and tilting his head meaningfully toward Sarah. "Promise."

Sarah walked through and Singer closed the door. Their breath steamed in the air.

"Looks like you made a connection," Sarah said.

He shrugged. "Only because you were there. I fit the profile of every john who comes to see her. She felt at least marginally safe with you in the room."

"Even though I'm a cop?" Sarah asked.

"Some things are more basic than that. If someone like me is in the room alone with her, she's either hooking or being raped or being beaten. With three of us—one of who is a woman and a cop—the dynamic changes and she can at least hope she's not going to get assaulted."

Sarah shivered and not because of the cold. "So what did she say?"

"We're on the right track. 'Daddy' is Tena, like you thought. He was the local pimp, the manager. Three or four girls stayed at his house. He dropped them here each afternoon if they weren't needed for a special arrangement, like a john that contacted him through the web or by e-mail. He took anything they could use to run. Or they weren't allowed to have it in the first place."

"Which is why we didn't find any coats or shoes."

"Right. They're stuck. He paid Paul to pick up their take once or twice a night so they wouldn't have any cash to leave with. Apparently, he'd also collect the phones each night and check the history. If he found the girls had called anyone but him, he'd beat the shit out of them. When he wasn't raping them, of course."

"Why do they put up with it? I thought the superpimp we're looking for sweet-talked them into hooking?" Sarah asked.

"To start with, maybe," Singer said. "But then he hands them over to Tena. A few weeks into hooking, they don't have any possessions or money and a guy who hits them if they talk back. Where are they going to go? Who are they going to complain to?"

"Lord," she said. The image of Tena's body sprawled on his kitchen floor didn't seem quite so horrible now. "What about the texts?"

"The girls get lonely between tricks, so they text each other. Which is why there are so many messages, from so many sources."

"And why they're all from the same date," Sarah said slowly, catching on. "They erase the text history each night."

"Yep. She said Tena would call each of them once or twice a night to make sure they were working or to set up a special meet with a john." Singer blew on his hands, then rubbed them together to warm them. "He let them text each other to keep them happy, but he didn't want them talking on the phone in case a john showed."

Sarah paused, thinking. "They're . . . prisoners. Slaves. No money, no way to communicate, no way to leave."

Singer nodded and motioned at the room. "There might as well be bars on the door."

"What about the mastermind, the one we're looking for? She mention him?"

He made a face. "She said she was the only one Tena had personally recruited, but the other girls talked about a guy named 'Eddie' nonstop."

"Eddie," she said, rolling the name around.

"I know," he said, seeing her look. "It's not exactly 'Hitler' or 'Dracula,' is it?"

"She have any idea where he is?"

"No. But she said Tena sounded weird on the phone when he called to check on her."

"Maybe after he called Eddie and told him about me," Sarah said.

"I think so," Singer said. "After you spooked Tena, he calls Eddie and tells him about you. Eddie, thinking fast, tells him, 'Stay put, I'll be there soon and we'll talk the situation over.' The girls were already here at the Crowne, so he was clear to ace Tena at home."

She thought about it, then sighed. "She's a dead end?"

He grimaced. "Maybe, though confirmation is always good. We were working on nothing but theories until now. But she doesn't know how to get ahold of Eddie or anyone besides Tena."

"Which is just how the pimps wanted it," she said. "But one of these girls, the ones Eddie recruited directly, has to know more about him. We need to keep knocking on doors until we find her."

Singer nodded, then a door opened above them. They craned their necks upward to see Rhee leaning over the railing, looking for them.

"Singer?"

"Over here. Got something?"

"Definitely maybe."

In the time it took the two of them to hotfoot it up the steps, Rhee had already tapped a cigarette out of its pack, lit it, and taken a drag. He blew a lungful into the night sky and used the top of the rail to knock off the first bit of ash. The bite of the match hung in the air.

"Why don't you tell me what you know so I don't repeat myself," he said as they topped the stairs. Sarah took turns with Singer filling in Rhee, who nodded from time to time. He smoked steadily and mechanically, finishing the cigarette as they offered him what they knew.

"Girl in here is named April," he said, flicking his butt into the parking lot. The cherry-red tip made an electric arc through the air. "Everything you said jibes with her story with one big difference."

"What's that?" Singer asked.

The Wicked Flee

"I'll let her tell you, see if you think what I'm thinking," Rhee said. He opened the unit door and they went in. The smell in here wasn't any better than in Trish's room, but at least it was warm.

Sitting in a chair, smoking her own cigarette, was a woman in her early twenties, with black roots showing through bottle-blonde hair. She wore spandex hot pants and a pink, short-sleeved shirt with a plunging V-neck. One leg was hooked over the arm of her chair so that her foot dangled, and she bobbed it up and down so that her flip-flop clapped gently against the sole of her foot. She gave the three of them a hard look as they trooped into the room.

"These your squad mates, honey?" she said. Her voice was scratchy.

"That's right," Rhee said. "Tell them what you told me."

"Since you asked so nicely," April said. "What do you want to know?"

"Rhee said you're different than the other girls here," Sarah said.

April shrugged. "Most all of these girls here are local, picked up by that asshole Eddie. Most are middle-class cuties, if you can believe it. Bowie. Columbia. Burtonsville. He promised to marry them or something."

"West and south of Baltimore, north of DC."

"Yeah," she said, then took a drag and blew it toward the ceiling. "But Eddie picked *me* up in Breezewood."

"Pennsylvania?" Sarah asked.

"You know another Breezewood, honey?"

"Town of Motels," Singer said.

April laughed, hoarse and grating, taken off guard. She pointed at Singer with her cigarette. "That's right. That sign on the turnpike. Town of Motels. Jesus."

"What's so special about Breezewood?" Sarah asked.

"Truckers," Singer said. "Steady source of clients where the turnpike and I-70 meet. Easy to get out of there and move on quickly. Cheap motels."

"Motels?" April said. "Who's going to pay for a motel? Everything happens in the cab."

"I stand corrected," Singer said, dryly.

"So the point is," Rhee said, impatient, "April was working a truck stop on her own. Eddie spotted her, asked if she wanted to make some real money, then brought her back here."

"What's the punch line?" Singer asked.

"Eddie already had a girl with him," April said. "But she *didn't* come back with us."

Singer arched an eyebrow and shot a glance at Chuck, but didn't say anything.

April continued. "Pretty little thing, cried the whole time when she wasn't doped to high hell. It was weird. Eddie drove around for a while with her bawling and me wondering what we're doing, then he dropped me off at a diner and told me to kill an hour. When he came back, the girl was gone, we drove to Maryland, and I started this illustrious career at the Huntington Crowne Motel."

"I can't say I'm happy I was right," Singer said.

Rhee nodded. "Eddie's working two games, like you thought. He runs strings of girls down here for the steady cash then grabs other girls for the occasional big score."

"He meets his clients in Breezewood so they can both get in and out easily," Sarah said. "Head west for three hours and you're in Ohio. Same thing east and you're crossing the New Jersey line. Philly in less than that."

Singer turned to April. "Did he have any other places he liked to go? Baltimore? New York? Richmond?"

She shrugged, stubbing her cigarette out on the arm of the chair. "No idea, hon. He didn't exactly confide in me and I haven't seen him since he dropped me here with that piece of shit Gerry."

Singer glanced at Rhee and made a face. Rhee nodded, running a hand through his hair. "I know. We got no proof he's heading back there. And Interstate 95 is just as easy to get to as I-70. We don't even know if he's heading north, for Christ's sake."

The three went quiet, each of them searching for a flaw in the logic, something that might give them the answer they needed, or at least eliminate one of the possibilities. Minutes passed. Finally, Singer spoke.

"Chuck, it doesn't matter where he *might* be. We've got nothing else to go on. Either he's on his way to Breezewood . . ."

"Or he's anywhere on the Eastern Seaboard," Rhee finished. "You're right. We gotta go." He turned to Sarah. "You in?"

She nodded. "Hell, yes."

He flashed a quick smile that disappeared so quickly she wasn't sure she'd seen it. "Thanks."

"What about the girls?" Singer asked. He canted his head toward April. "Does she know about . . . ?"

"Does she know about what?" April asked, suspicious.

"Uh," Rhee said, turning toward her. "Your pal Eddie decided to downsize his staff earlier tonight."

"What the hell does that mean?"

"He put two bullets in the back of Gerry's head."

"Oh," April said, taken aback.

"And I'm going to do something similar to Eddie, if I catch him. So, you all can do whatever you want now."

"You're not going to run us in?" she asked.

"Shit," he said. "This ain't no bust. I'm after my sister and that's it. If you and the other girls can get out of here, do it."

"How the hell are we supposed to do that? You think I got a trust fund up my—"

"Probably not," Sarah interrupted, then pulled out her business card. She flipped it over and wrote a number on the back. "Here. This is the number for a friend of mine named Jimmy. He's a cop, but he's not going to be interested in running you in. He'll at least give you and the other girls a ride to an Amtrak or Greyhound station."

"Wait," Singer said. "Don't go there. Let me see that card." He scribbled something below Jimmy's number. "This is the name and number for my daughter, Amanda. She helps direct a women's shelter in DC called FirstStep. I'll call and tell her to expect you. Get Trooper Haynesworth's friend to drive you there. Amanda will take care of you."

April took the card with a look that spoke for itself.

"It's not like you'd expect. They can help you find work, a place to sleep, and training if you need it. Oh, and take this." Singer stepped forward and handed her a roll of bills.

"What's this?"

"The night manager's cut for the week," Singer said. "I kind of figured this is where we'd finish and, uh, convinced him it might be worth his time to make a donation. I'm going to give the other girls their share and then you call that number."

April stared at the wad of bills and the card like they were diamonds, shaking her head. Her eyes were shiny.

"You're welcome," Singer said, smiling.

"We done here?" Chuck asked, fidgeting by the door.

"I think so," Singer said, then cracked his knuckles. "Let's go get Lucy."

CHAPTER TWENTY-EIGHT

The girl wouldn't stop crying and it was driving him insane.

When Lucy had seen his face, she'd freaked out and tried to rush past him, kicking and screaming until he'd pinned her to the passenger's seat. Even then, she'd landed a kick to the inside of his thigh that still ached and when he'd reached in to grab her, she'd pulled a goddamn knife out of thin air and nearly ended him. Doris had grabbed her arm at the last second and kept the thing from going into his eye.

He squeezed her wrist until she'd dropped the knife, but it still had taken both of them to get her under control, Eddie holding her down while Doris held her bunched-up coat over the girl's mouth and nose until she started passing out. It was the only way to teach her a lesson without leaving a mark. When it finally sunk in that they'd let her breathe if she'd sit quietly, they'd bundled her into the Mustang and shut the door.

As a thank-you, he'd paid Doris a flat five hundred bucks from Gerry's stash, told her to go home and see if Jack was still alive, and promised to send the full payment despite Jack being his typical numbskull self and letting the girl escape. It had been just his luck that Doris had been out partying when he'd brought Lucy around for safekeeping. The girl had probably clocked Jack with one of his own stupid replica weapons and trussed him like a turkey ten minutes after getting dropped off. If Doris had been there instead, he could've rested easy, knowing that things would be taken care of.

Doris had been his helper for the past two years and was worth more than Gerry, Jack, and every other knucklehead he'd worked with combined. She had a sharp mind and an empathy she could turn on and off when she needed to. He'd sent her to Gerry and the other managers from time to time to calm the girls down or explain the finer points of pimping. The girls trusted her and lapped up the bullshit she spun about making enough money to leave the life or kick their habit or find a better way, while guys like Gerry got put in their place in record time if they thought they'd push Doris around. She'd slipped a knife into Gerry's pants once to remind him—in case he'd forgotten—which ones were the whores and which one wasn't. Sometimes Eddie thought the guys were more scared of her than him.

He could've used Doris now with Lucy's nonstop moaning and crying. He considered force-feeding her some of the roofies he kept on hand and doping her into silence. If not, it was going to be a long drive.

The entire situation had already shredded his nerves and he was sweating and jittery, unable to concentrate on the road. Which sucked, because driving was one of the few things that he did to calm down. At this point, however, he was ready to pop. He'd taken the gun out of its hiding place in the armrest and instead kept it in the crease between his seat and the center console. He didn't know why he'd put it there and was too scared to analyze it any further. All he knew was that he'd never be able to bluff his way through another encounter with a cop like he'd done earlier in the night. He was so on edge that a cop could ask him his name and he'd probably get it wrong.

"Shut *up*," he shouted as Lucy groaned again. "I swear to God I'll beat the living shit out of you, you don't shut up. I don't care how much money I lose, you understand?"

The moaning died down, but Lucy said, "Why are you doing this?"

He glanced at her. Her eyes were bright red around the dark black-brown irises and her nose was red and glistening. She looked like a little girl and he turned his gaze back at the road. "For money. Why do you think?"

"But . . . it's my life," she whispered. "You're ruining my life."

"Your life isn't worth shit next to mine, okay?" he said. "I don't know you and I don't want to know you. I don't care about you and I'm not going to care. You don't matter to me. Everyone thinks they're special, that bad things can't happen to them or their family. Until it does and then life gets real, fast."

Lucy sniffled but didn't say anything.

"It's funny how everyone thinks they've got the right to do what they want, live how they want. They think they're *owed*, that they *deserve* a comfortable ride. When disaster strikes, somehow it's not fair, it's a mistake." Eddie's voice rose to a mocking falsetto. "This is someone else's problem . . . what am I doing with it?"

He thought for a moment, his eyes following the road in front of them, but not seeing it. "Life is shit. You do what you can with it. You grab what you can, when you can, or someone else takes it from you. Plus a little extra. And if that happens to you, you deserved it."

They were both quiet for a second. Lucy wiped the back of her hand across her nose and swallowed a few times. "Why don't you do something different, be somebody different? My parents were killed in a car wreck. My brother and I—"

"I don't care," Eddie interrupted. "Understand? I . . . don't . . . care. I don't give a shit that you pulled yourself up by your bootstraps or your brother is living the American Dream or your family found Jesus and is born again. I. Don't. Care."

Lucy shrank back in her seat, silent. The only sound was the tires on the road and his own ragged breathing. He felt like he'd run a marathon. His hands were sore from squeezing the steering wheel, and a dull ache that had started at the base of his neck was now progressing through the rest of his head, threatening to blow it off.

A memory teased him. Late fall or early winter. He was cold, because the utility company had turned the heat off earlier in the week. His mother, standing by the window, arms crossed, smoking. Waiting. Watching the street. Eddie sat on the grubby suede couch, watching her, too scared to move or say anything. When she finished one cigarette, she would reach over to the TV where she'd set the pack down, pluck out another and light it, then slap the lighter down and go back to looking out the window.

She'd stayed that way for hours. The light outside began to fade, then died completely. Finally, the streetlights came on and she turned around from the window as though that had been the sign she'd been waiting for all along.

"Well," she said. Resigned. Tired. "I guess your daddy's not coming home."

She went into the kitchen and poured herself a shot of vodka from the bottle of Aristocrat they kept on top of the refrigerator. Three nights later, she sent him out to play at a friend's house all day. Two weeks later, she told him to go play outside after it was already dark. It was when he came back because he was so cold he couldn't feel his toes that he saw a strange man coming out of the house.

He refused to look at Lucy. "My dad was a junkie and weighed a hundred pounds when he died in an alley in Cherry Hill. My mom fucked for food so I wouldn't have to. And if I didn't do what I do to survive, then and now, I'd be dead or wishing to God I was," he said in a hoarse voice.

Lucy stared at him, scared into silence.

"You're merchandise. That's all you are. If you find a way out later, on your own time, more power to you. You try to run out on me now, I'll kill you. See the difference? If I don't protect me and mine, that's the same as flushing it down the tubes. And that isn't going to happen. Now, sit back and shut up."

CHAPTER TWENTY-NINE

There was a time for jokes. To take people's minds off their troubles, to let the air out of a tense situation, to gently and diplomatically express a different viewpoint. Then there were times when humor could only do damage and the joke you thought would be the perfect icebreaker turned out to be the worst possible idea. The line between was thin and always shifting.

Take, for instance, the situation I was in, riding shotgun with Chuck driving while Trooper First Class Haynesworth followed us in her cruiser. Chuck, who *normally* drove at twice the recommended speed limit, was pushing the upper range of just how fast a modified Acura Integra could go and still stay on the ground. And I think he was only going as slow as he was out of consideration for me. His concentration was absolute. His face, in profile, appeared to be carved out of granite.

It seemed to be the wrong moment for humor.

The Wicked Flee

Still, it might be worth one last joke before I died. I was gripping what we called, in high school, the "chicken bar" or the "oh-shit handle," struggling to look nonchalant as we outraced the Integra's headlights and for sure Chuck's ability to brake in a reasonable manner. Instinctively, my feet had wedged themselves in opposite corners of the passenger's-side foot well, bracing for what I believed was our inevitable wreck.

One consolation was that only two of us would go out in a blaze of glory, since Sarah wasn't in the backseat. I was happy she was following. First, she didn't have to feel she was playing second fiddle to the two of us. And, second, if we got to Breezewood and found out that information we'd teased out of April had only been half right, we'd need all the legwork we could get to search the Town of Motels. And, third, of course, she might be the only survivor of the road trip.

In the end, I decided the last thing we needed was a joke. Chuck had a decent sense of humor, but this was a serious situation and one that might end badly. I respected that and we'd been quiet, watching the Maryland countryside fly by for long minutes, when he suddenly spoke.

"Hey," he said, breaking the silence.

"Yeah?"

"How many mice does it take to screw in a lightbulb?"

I looked over at him, not sure I'd heard correctly. "What?"

"How many mice does it take to screw in a lightbulb?"

Eyebrows raised, I said, "I don't know, Chuck. How many?"

"Two. If they're small enough."

I stared at him, amazed, not sure how to respond.

He glanced over, giving me a weak smile. "You looked pretty serious. Thought I'd lighten the mood."

I shook my head. "As jokes go, it's weak tea, but I'll take it."

The smile grew into a grin, but it faded quickly. "Hey, back there at the motel. I'm sorry."

"What do you mean?"

"Hitting that guy. Paul," he said. We hadn't shifted gears in thirty miles, but Chuck rested his hand on the stick shift anyway. "I know you know, but I wanted to put it out there—I'm not that kind of cop."

"Really? I thought you guys in Gangs all worked that way," I said. "You know, 'If you can't join 'em, beat 'em.' That kind of thing."

He shot me a look, making me wonder once again about the judicious use of humor in stressful situations, but the grin flashed back on, then off again. "We never hit our suspects. You never know when you might need to score a couple of tickets to a Wizards game from the guy in the chair."

I laughed and something bad went away. I knew Chuck was a good cop and that the episode back at the motel had been under exceptional circumstances, but it was nice to know he wanted to get it out on the table and square things with me.

"Changing the subject, what do you think of . . . ?" He jerked a thumb behind us.

"Trooper First Class?" I asked. "Smart, competent. Definitely more with it than I was at her age."

"That's not saying much."

"Granted. Her initiative makes me curious, though. It's clear she's moonlighting."

"Good for her," Chuck said. "What's wrong with that?"

"Nothing, as far as I'm concerned, although working in Gangs might've screwed with your sense of proper departmental conduct. But she's, what, twenty-four? Would you have felt okay working off the clock with only a year or two under your belt?"

Chuck pursed his lips. "Gangs is different than normal police work. Sometimes it's as much life as job. So, yeah, I would've scratched around here or there, maybe. You need to exercise a little ambition if you don't want to walk a beat the rest of your life. But I see what you mean."

"Question is, is that a good thing or a bad thing?" I asked.

"Like, is she a glory hound?"

"Something like that."

He considered it, then shook his head. "Don't think so. She adjusted quickly to a screwy situation at the motel, then chipped in when we started quizzing the girls. She seems like she wants some answers, not a chance to grandstand."

I nodded. "I thought so, too. Just wanted to get your take on it."

We hit an uphill slope and Chuck downshifted to fourth. The needle redlined on the RPMs and the engine screamed, but we took the hill at ninety. Before you could get through the opening line of the Gettysburg Address, we'd plateaued and were back in fifth gear.

"Question," Chuck said after a minute.

"Answer," I said.

"We're chasing this guy Eddie, but what about the guy he's meeting?"

"What about him?"

"There are a couple of scenarios," Chuck said, clearing his throat. "Best case, we get there in time and nab both of them. Life is good and we go home."

"Okay."

"The other possibility, we get there too late for the exchange, but we catch Eddie."

"Or worst case, we get there too late, and we miss both Eddie and this guy," I said, because one of us had to.

"Right. What are our options in each case?"

The question was rhetorical—Chuck knew as well as I did what we would do—but I ran through the list as an exercise. "In the best case, we get Lucy back. Life is good and, if we're feeling charitable, we hand the two scumbags over to Sarah so she can get credit for the collar. We'll be pulled in to testify, but whatever."

"Uh-huh."

"You and Sarah might get a slap on the wrist for, uh, exercising your ambitions outside jurisdictional lines, but nobody's going to complain too much."

"Right."

"In the worst-case scenario," I said, slowly—it was not a pretty thought—"we'll need help. Every state cop in Maryland, Pennsylvania, and probably West Virginia, Ohio, and New Jersey will have to be on the lookout for one or both of them. Maybe we can help Sarah chase down more of this superpimp's network and get a plate to chase or a cell phone to tap. Find one of the other managers like this guy Gerry and lean on him. Pull on a string and maybe we can get someone to roll on him if we pull hard enough."

"Okay," he said. "What if we get the middle scenario?"

"Like?"

"What if we get to Breezewood but snag just one of them?"

"And Lucy's with the other guy? Okay, then we have to work quickly and get whoever we have in custody to cough up some intel on the other one."

"What if we can't convince him to talk?"

I hesitated. "Then we're . . . well, we're essentially back in worst-case-scenario territory and we'll have to call in the cavalry."

"By then, it'll be too late," Chuck said matter-of-factly, though I knew it cost him to say it.

I took a deep breath and nodded.

"So, the reason I asked is," he said, choosing his words carefully, "we got a clear course of action in both the best and the worst situations. No questions, just do this, do that, and go with it."

"Yeah."

"But the situation in the middle is . . . dicey. We spend too long asking one of these guys who, what, and where and I—" His breath caught and he coughed. "I might not see Lucy again."

I nodded, finally seeing where this was going. "On the other hand, this might all have a happy ending if we get the information we need."

"Right," he said and we were quiet for a full minute or more. I looked out my window. The orange glow of lamplight in the distance spoke of homes and families safe in their beds, their lives serene, quiet, and untouched as we flew through the night.

In the window's reflection, I saw Chuck glance at me, then turn back to the road. "What I'm saying is, if we catch one of these guys, but not the other, I'm going to do whatever it takes to find Lucy. I can't afford to play nice. I can't let the middle scenario turn into the worst case. I need you to understand that."

"You're asking if I disapprove?" No answer. I looked over. Chuck's face was stony. "No, you want to know if I'm going to stop you."

He nodded.

I looked out the window, thinking about lines I'd crossed in my past. Memories of those events had less to do with whether what I'd done had been right in the general sense of the word and more to do with if I'd regretted it in retrospect, if time and perspective had justified a choice that had felt wrong at the time. "Good people do bad things. Sometimes bad people do the opposite."

"Then how do you measure it? You break a guy's arm to get a confession, you're a bad cop. And I believe that. But, tonight, if we catch one of these guys and that's the only way to get Lucy back, I'll break every bone in his body."

I took a deep breath and leaned back in the seat. "This stuff is always a matter of degree. The questions we should be asking are, how often do we do this? How far are we willing to go? For what reasons?"

"And do you have a choice," he said.

I nodded, reluctantly. We were attempting to rationalize something ugly and dangerous. It was slippery moral ground, and I thought I knew where I stood on the issue. I'd been involved in plenty of uncertain situations where a modicum of persuasion would've gone a long way toward getting the truth.

I'd also seen it used for lousy reasons, too, like to save time or because it felt good to some cops to beat the hell out of the bad guys. Observe that enough, though, and you realize you need to step back, think on it, and make a personal decision before the situation happens again. Because if you rely on the heat of the moment to guide you, you'll make the worst choice, every time. Upon reflection, I'd decided early on, like Chuck, that I wasn't going to be that kind of cop and if I had to take the long way around to get to the finish line, then that's how it was going to have to be.

But we weren't talking abstractions right now. We were discussing what lengths we were willing to go—maybe by the end of the night—to save someone's life. And not just anyone, somebody Chuck knew. Someone he loved. What would I do if it was Amanda?

"So what does all that add up to?" he asked after a minute. "I already know I'm going to do whatever it takes to get Lucy back. But how do I wrap my head around what I'm willing to do? What's righteous and what's not? Where's the line?"

"You won't know where the line is until you've crossed it," I said. Then we both fell silent, because it was a terrible answer, but the only one we had.

CHAPTER THIRTY

The twin taillights of Rhee's Integra were bright red rubies a hundred feet in front of her, twisting and blending at times into four, then six, and back to two again as her eyes lost their focus, the lids lowered gently—then snapped open again as Sarah caught herself dozing off. If there was anything more monotonous than following another car at four in the morning with the snow coming down in an endless, curving waterfall in front of you, Sarah hadn't seen it.

Rhee was pushing triple-digit speeds but, like anything else, extremes became the norm and soon cruising at almost a hundred miles an hour seemed as ho-hum as fifty-five. The landscape was still shrouded in darkness, and traffic was sparse enough that she didn't have a frame of reference. The only clue she had for how fast they were going was when they approached a car doing the speed limit, overtook it in a blink, and left it behind faster than thought.

Fast was fine with her, since she didn't know how much time she had. Technically, this was her day off, but all state troopers were on call and with weather this bad, it wouldn't be unusual to get a call telling her to hoof it back to Waterloo. Double-time-and-a-half pay, and that was great, but she'd have to tell Rhee and Singer that they were on their own. They'd understand—hell, they'd probably be relieved—but she could kiss her moonlighting case good-bye. Rhee was a good cop and Singer appeared to be cut from the same cloth, but their primary goal was to get Rhee's sister back and if that meant letting the pimp off in exchange for Lucy, they'd do it without hesitation.

She couldn't blame them. But what about the rest of the girls, the ones she knew and the ones she didn't? Tiffany had been somebody's baby girl. And maybe Trish was someone's sister. And next month there'd be another girl in their place. If she threw away a chance to break up the network, there wasn't anyone left to rescue those girls.

She scrubbed her face with one hand, willing some of her energy to return. She was going to pay for this later, she knew. Fingers crossed she wouldn't get that call from the barracks. Because, if she did, she'd be pulling what amounted to seventy-two hours on the job with three hours of sleep. And then it wouldn't be long before *she'd* be the one needing roadside assistance.

As if on cue, her phone gave a jangle, making her jump. She fished it out of her pocket and the bottom of her stomach hit the floor. Waterloo Barracks. For a brief, ridiculous moment, she considered not answering the call, then discarded the idea. One did *not* ignore calls from one's HQ. She groaned, thinking. What were the chances that it was just Jimmy, impatient and wanting an update on where her "case" was going?

She pushed the little green button. "Haynesworth."

There was a slight pause, then the voice she dreaded to hear came over the line. "Trooper, where are you, exactly?"

"Lieutenant Kline," she said, feeling a sensation like cold water rushing over her body. "How are you?"

"I'm doing fine, Trooper. Thank you so much for inquiring," Kline said. "I'll ask you again. Where are you?"

She swallowed. "In my cruiser, sir."

"And where is your cruiser?"

"Thirty-five miles south of Breezewood, Lieutenant."

"I see," he said. "And are you southbound?"

She gave a mental sigh. "No, sir. North."

"Is there any particular reason why you're pointed towards the Pennsylvania Turnpike at four o'clock in the morning on your day off?"

She was quiet.

"Goddamn it, Sarah," Kline exploded. "I don't know what the hell to do with you. You're a good officer. You're smart and dedicated and you've got tons of potential. But just how stupid do you think I am? Thirty minutes after you left Glenwood, Jay Saunders called me and told me you'd been sniffing around his murder case. Did you think he was going to swallow your story whole? Without checking with me?"

"No, sir. I guess not."

"I sat here in the dark for damn near two hours, wondering how to handle this," he said. Sarah said nothing and he sighed. "Tell me everything. Now."

So she gave him everything she'd put together. She described the extemporaneous interrogation of Handley in the car to her attempt to shake down Tena. He grunted when she mentioned Rhee and Singer—it didn't seem prudent to leave them out of the narrative—and finished with what they were planning to do in Breezewood.

He swore, then sighed again. "What a mess. Two cops out of their jurisdiction and an armed civilian, all on a crusade. You couldn't wait for Glenwood PD to chase this down? Report it to the state troopers in PA and let them intercept?"

Sarah took a deep breath. "The girl is in a car heading there right now, sir. Rhee and Singer feel she's going to be off our radar in a matter of hours. Maybe already is. After what I've seen, I agree with them. But it wouldn't matter if I was in or not—they'd be doing this without me. In any case, this may be a chance to grab the head of this network, the one who put these strings of girls together."

"And that's worth it to you?"

"Yes, sir. All the way."

A sleepy murmur on the other end of the line interrupted them. Kline's hand muffled the phone, and she heard him say, "Something came up, Mary. Go back to bed. I'll be there in a second."

The hand moved away from the phone and Kline's voice was back, strong and decisive. "All right, Trooper. Here's the deal. As of twelve-oh-one this morning, you're on the record as taking one day of personal leave. Anything you do from that point onward in the next twenty-four hours, short of shooting someone, is your business."

She was quiet.

"But Waterloo and your commanding officer," he continued, "are not part of what you do on your own time. You do not have sanction. Do something stupid and I'll hang you out to dry. I will not let your adventuring tarnish the reputation of the Waterloo Barracks or the Maryland State Police. Understood?"

She caught herself nodding up and down. "Yes, sir."

He paused, as though expecting an argument from her. "As far as I'm concerned, you're back in the fold in twenty-*five* hours from midnight tonight. If I catch you working this . . . case while you're on duty, you'll be a security guard at Arundel Mills Mall for the rest of your days. If you find evidence of a crime being committed, we'll follow through on your leads via the proper channels."

"I understand, sir."

"And one more thing."

"Sir?"

"Tell Noles I'm holding him personally responsible for your conduct. There's no way you would've followed through on this without him egging you on."

"Yes, sir."

Kline hung up without another word, but she kept the phone glued to her ear for another ten seconds just in case, then eventually let her hand sink to her lap. Her heart was actually pounding in her chest. Not because she was afraid of Kline, necessarily, but because it had become very clear, very quickly, that her career had hung in the balance on this one phone call. One wrong word and, in an alternate universe, another Sarah Haynesworth was turning the car around and driving to Waterloo Barracks to clean out her desk. But that's not how it happened here.

A smile broke across her face. Kline couldn't fool her. If he'd truly been upset, he would've terminated her right over the phone. He couldn't say so, of course, but in so many words, he'd admitted his own shortsightedness and given her permission to follow the case. In fact, she'd better bring back a trophy or two or he'd be disappointed. She was on a short leash—*twenty-four hours*—but he'd had every right to tell her to return for a full reprimand. The fact that he hadn't spoke volumes.

No longer fighting sleep, she slipped the phone in her pocket, put both hands on the steering wheel, and pressed down on the gas until she was almost on top of the Integra. Rhee was going to have to pick it up if they were going to solve this thing in a day.

CHAPTER THIRTY-ONE

The approach to Breezewood was a long, darkened slope more than a mile long. The only traffic for an hour had been convoys of semitrucks, as many as twelve at once, saving time on their thousand-mile journeys by driving through the middle of the night when there were only a handful of cars on the road. The trucks, when they passed, were like walls, towering over the Mustang. Except these walls were steel and rubber and glass moving at eighty miles an hour on the flats and closer to ninety-five on the downhill side.

The shuddering blare of the air brakes as the truckers tried to rein it in sounded like the end of the world when it happened right next to you. All Eddie could do—with his nerves already ground down to nothing—was grit his teeth, squeeze the wheel, and wait for them to pass. Normally he was a competent, confident driver, but the situation was hardly normal and it wasn't helped by either the truckers or the snow whipping head-on into his windshield.

The Wicked Flee

Lucy hadn't said a word since his little tell-all. That suited him fine, though his admission had cut deeper into his own psyche than he'd thought possible. He wasn't afraid of his past or even ashamed of it, but it was the first time he'd ever even mentioned his parents to anyone, let alone a girl he was getting ready to sell like a cut of meat. It made him wonder what might've happened if even one of his parents had been remotely normal. Would he have stayed in school, or gotten married, or turned out just like them? Would he have bought his ticket in some back alley of Baltimore, looking to score just one more hit? Or would he have worked past all that and become one of the good guys, teaching or counseling or writing poetry?

His small laugh brought on by *that* idea made the fantasy evaporate like smoke. This was why he hardly ever dreamed of something bigger or better. He had never had the chance, so why even wonder? He was a pimp, a supplier of women to an insatiable and unquestioning public. He had plans, sure, and they didn't always involve selling girls, but he had no delusions about who he was . . . or what he was good at.

Orange lights blinking with a slow, steady pulse appeared at the bottom of the hill, signaling to drivers to reduce their speed. Rumble strips reinforced the concept for the drivers too headstrong to pay attention to signs, shaking their cars like a jackhammer had been let loose in the trunk. Brake lights winked cherry red as traffic eased to a stop at the light guarding the entrance to Breezewood proper. The line of cars and trucks curved gently to the right as they queued for their opportunity to pass through the town and on to their final destination.

Breezewood, for as long as Eddie had known it, had always been just a strip of fast-food joints, gas stations, and trucker hotels on either side of the road that connected Interstate 70 with the Pennsylvania Turnpike. At a little under a mile long, with the southernmost entrance to the turnpike just around the corner, it should've taken most travelers a few minutes to get through, but six lights and the intersection of two states' worth of traffic often meant a half-hour wait to discover the other side of town. But Eddie wasn't interested in simply passing through.

What he was looking for was the run-down face of the Calloway Motel. The Calloway had been around since the sixties at least, and hadn't been updated, renovated, or probably cleaned since then. Between the bedbugs, the junkies, and the moldering walls, it was safer to grab a cot at the county jail than spend a night at the Calloway. All of which made it the perfect location for illicit activity of any kind. The same level of isolation and disrepair that kept any sane customer away meant there were few eyes, fewer lights, and no cameras.

Eddie made a careful turn left as the majority of traffic veered right through the strip and on to get a bite to eat or continued up the hill to catch the on-ramp for the turnpike. The beat-down motel wasn't on the actual strip—the rent was too high and the urban blight had barely existed when the Calloway had been built, anyway. He made a quick turn onto Graceville Road and a minute later the Mustang was pulling into the modest parking lot for the Calloway, a cinder field situated atop a small rise that looked down on the glitz and glamour of sandwich shops and diesel pumps.

Taking his time, he circled the parking lot twice, looking for signs of life, but even for the Calloway, it was dead. Puzzled, he peered at the building, hoping to see a solitary light or closing blind—then the handwritten "OUT OF BUSINESS" sign tacked to the door told the story. He rolled up the window, a sour expression on his face. So that was the end of the Calloway . . . and the end of him using it as a place for his transactions. Then he reminded himself—he wouldn't need it after tonight. Maybe fate had shut down the old fleabag motel. It had simply jumped the gun by a few days.

Whatever the reason, the Calloway was now the wrong place to do the swap. It was familiar and isolated, but if a cop—and there were as many state police as local pigs in a town intersected by three or four highways—caught the flash of headlights or even the glint off a fender, there'd be a cruiser climbing the hill to investigate a minute later. For all he knew, cops did an hourly drive-by to make sure no one was doing exactly what Eddie was planning. He couldn't take a chance on either case. He had to find a new place to make the sale.

Easing the Mustang over to the edge of the parking lot, he got a good look down onto the business district of Breezewood. Past the rusted guardrail at the edge of the lot where cans and bags and soda bottles had been marooned, the entire strip spread out below him—parking lots, gas stations, restaurants, convenience stores. In most towns, businesses would still be hours from opening, but people who made their living on the highway didn't keep nine-to-five schedules and already there was movement around most of the storefronts. The question was, where could they go that wasn't too busy *or* too dead to make the exchange?

There. From his vantage point, Eddie could see the entire profile of a truckers' rest stop, the one they called the On Ramp. He wondered why he hadn't thought of it before. It was the last major business for drivers heading for the turnpike toll station, so it had a sprawling car and RV parking lot in the front that served a huge two-story complex of fast-food kiosks, bathrooms, and gift shops. To tempt the truckers, however, the back of the business—a huge, multiacre lot—was reserved parking for the big rigs, with pull-through stalls to make it easy on them, and special bathroom and shower facilities reserved for truckers. With most of the cabs having their own sleeping quarters, there wasn't any reason to have a separate motel, but the long-haulers liked to get a shower and a bite without having to wade through a sea of tourists.

They also liked to get laid, which is how Eddie knew about it. The truckers' lot of the On Ramp is where he'd pimped out some of his first girls after leaving Carolyn Park. It was as simple as dropping off three or four girls in the back, parking the Mustang in the front, then going inside for coffee. He'd kill three or four hours on his phone or reading the paper, then he'd hop in the Mustang, gather the girls, and drive them to a nearby apartment or trailer before starting all over the next night. He'd left money on the table leaving after only a few hours, but truck stops were also the favorite place for state cops to stage a raid, so it didn't hurt to get out while he was ahead.

The best part was that the On Ramp's management knew exactly what was going on, but they also knew it was a service the truckers expected. So there were no cameras covering the rear lot except those pointed at the back door for basic security. And Eddie knew from experience that they did their best to flick the lights or send out a manager to warn them if they'd heard a raiding party was on its way.

As long as he stayed away from the doors and didn't attract any attention, he could make the swap with Torbett in the middle of the busiest business in Breezewood. As long as his client didn't freak out at the latest change in plans, this chapter of his life would close before sunrise, and he'd be heading north with a suitcase full of cash, ready to start his life over.

CHAPTER THIRTY-TWO

Already on edge from the night's numerous mistakes, Torbett nearly jumped out of his skin when #5 rang. The insistent electronic beeping went off just as he caught sight of the first green highway sign for Breezewood.

"What now?" he asked in greeting. He was past bothering with any of his normal precautions.

"First, nothing is wrong," Eddie said, his voice tinny as it came over #5's cheap wiring. "I just want to be cautious."

"Admirable," Torbett said dryly.

"The Calloway is closed. They must've gone belly-up since the last time we met. Windows are boarded and there's nobody in the parking lot. Two cars meeting, even for a few minutes, might attract attention."

"What do you suggest?"

"There's a truckers' rest stop, the On Ramp, near the entrance to the turnpike. You'll see it right after you exit. The front is for tourists, mainly, but the back is truckers only. I've been there before and I know there aren't any cameras."

"If it's for trucks only, we'll stick out worse than if we were in an empty parking lot," Torbett said, alarmed. "And all it takes is some trucker taking a cell phone video of the exchange and we'll be screwed."

"Cars are allowed in the back. They just don't go here often. I know the lot because I used to supply girls to the truckers there."

"Fantastic. Then they know your car."

"I drove a different car then. And truckers don't take videos for kicks. They're either too tired, too drunk, or too busy screwing a hooker," Eddie said, his voice calm. "Look, this is a simple change to the plan, probably safer than meeting at the Calloway, even when it *was* open. This early in the morning, there'll be just enough people to give us some cover, but they'll all be too tired to notice what we're doing. I'll be waiting for you. You pull in beside me, we make the trade, and we're both back on the road in thirty seconds. Guaranteed."

Torbett was dead quiet, driving by reflex and barely aware of the road stretching ahead into the darkness. A nugget of dread was crawling through his gut, an indicator of his own instinct—an instinct that he never ignored. Survival to this point, while indulging in a hobby that was dangerous and monumentally illegal, had been due to caution so extreme that even paranoiacs would think he was crazy. Planning, redundant and overlapping precautions, and attention to detail were ninety-nine percent of it. One percent was gut instinct. And it was that reptilian-brained intuition that was telling him to look for the nearest break in the road so that he could turn around and head right back from where he'd come. *Now.*

"Look, I—"

"Hold on," Eddie said, interrupting him. "There's someone who wants to say hi."

A scuffling noise followed, the sound of someone lifting the phone away and passing it along. There was some unintelligible murmuring, then the sound of a short breath.

"Hello?"

Torbett closed his eyes, drinking in the sound like water. The voice was velvet-soft and high-pitched. The voice you'd expect to emanate from a doll or a fawn or an angel. A voice he wanted to hear every night, that would talk to him on command. A voice that would be his.

"Hello?" she said again. More murmuring in the background. A questioning uplift in the voice. An answer. Then he heard her mouth close to the phone and she said, "Steve?"

He stifled a groan, picturing her. Eddie's photo had been of poor quality and just a single image but, coupled with the voice, was enough to cause his heart to bang against his chest.

"Is this Lucy?"

"Yes—"

More scuffling noises. Eddie's voice came back on the line. "What do you think?"

Torbett swallowed. The muscles in his neck were strained. He shoved down the internal ranting of the reptilian-brained survivalist and accepted the risk—not that he had a choice. Someone else's hands were on the wheel now, someone else's brain was making the calculations to Breezewood, someone else's voice was saying, "Where do you want to meet, again?"

He could hear Eddie's voice, smug and confident. Torbett didn't care. "The On Ramp. You'll see it across the road a minute after you exit the turnpike. You can't miss it."

"I'll be there," he whispered, and ended the call.

CHAPTER THIRTY-THREE

Snow was flying sideways by the time we pulled onto Breezewood's main corridor of restaurants and gas stations. Visibility went from zero to two hundred feet based entirely on what direction the wind blew. Piercing white lights of fluorescent signs and multicolored sale banners showed us the way to an all-night doughnut shop parking lot, where Chuck swung into an open space. A second later, Sarah pulled her cruiser next to us. I rolled down my window and signaled for her to join us. She got out, her shoulders hunched against the cold, and opened the back door to the Integra. The blast of cold made me wince.

"A doughnut shop?" Sarah asked as she slid into the backseat. "Are you serious?"

"Habit," Chuck said, then turned sideways to include her in the conversation. "Let's put our heads together. We know anything about this guy besides the fact he's driving a black Mustang? Like, where he might be meeting? Tell me I missed something."

"What do we think we know?" I asked.

"They need a place that's easy on, easy off," Sarah said immediately. "It won't be far from the entrance to the turnpike; otherwise, why meet here? They'll want a quick exchange so they can get on their way."

"Agreed," I said. "So we start on the strip and work our way out."

"Does he want a place that's crowded or not?" Chuck asked. "Does he want to use traffic for cover or the back of a gas station to avoid witnesses?"

"It's almost five in the morning," I said. "Most places qualify as deserted."

"Not really," Sarah said, tilting her head toward the main drag. "Truckers and snowbirds are getting an early start. A few will even be finishing breakfast and hitting the road soon."

"Whatever. What's his thinking?" Chuck asked, impatient.

"I'd want activity," I said, "but nothing too transient. A gas station has a lot of people, but they're coming and going too quickly. A Mustang hanging around with a girl in the backseat or kicking in the trunk is going to attract attention. I'd pick a fast-food place, maybe with a side lot or a drive-thru that circles around back."

"They'll want to avoid security, though," Sarah said. "And those kind of places have cameras and some kind of system covering the back door."

"Hotels or motels?" I suggested. "There'd be enough cars to make it look busy and they might have cameras on the doors, but none of the flophouses around here have the budget to maintain surveillance on an entire parking lot."

"Makes sense," Chuck said.

Sarah had her smartphone out and was tapping away. "There are . . . five motels in a one-mile radius."

"What about restaurants?" Chuck asked over his shoulder.

"Depends on your definition," she said, studying the map. "Including fast-food joints and coffee shops, maybe a dozen? But everything's compact to take advantage of the turnpike traffic. And the motel locations overlap with the food, naturally, to nab the overnighters."

"That's it?" I asked. "Everything Breezewood has to offer is less than a mile away?"

"There are . . . let's see, two or three spurs off of the main drag. Probably where the town's expanded and a few old run-down places where the new construction has passed them by. We should be able to see them from the road."

"Anything we're missing?" Chuck asked.

I chewed my lip. "Rest stops that don't fit either description. There's one by the turnpike entrance, I forget the name. And a Flying J on the east end of town, although they cater to truckers. We passed it on the way in."

"That looked more like a gas station with a convenience store," Sarah said.

"Still might be worth checking out," I said.

"We gotta get going," Chuck said. "I'd rather cover some ground than think this to death. Sarah, you want to take the south side of the strip, at the west end? I'll do the other end and we'll work our way towards each other."

"Got it. We should try those spur roads, too, if they've got a business on them," she said. "Singer, you staying with Rhee?"

"Yeah," I said. "You know this area better than we do, so it might take both of us to catch something."

"You got our cell numbers," Chuck said. "Call if you see something, touch base in thirty minutes if you don't. If you find Eddie, don't move on him without us."

Sarah nodded and left, throwing a "Good luck" over her shoulder as she jumped out of Chuck's car and into the cruiser, ducking the biggest flakes. She started the cruiser, the headlights flashed on, then she turned left out of the parking lot. Chuck put his Integra in gear and we took a right, heading in the opposite direction down the stretch of lights, cars, and snow.

We were silent as we concentrated on the darkened storefronts and shadowed driveways, but it was difficult to believe the mutual silence wasn't hiding an unpleasant truth. Namely, that the odds of uncovering the proverbial needle-in-a-haystack were better than our chances of finding Lucy.

Maybe it wasn't that bad. In one regard, the odds were with us. We had decent information that we were in the right place at roughly the right time. Breezewood was a tiny town with a minuscule permanent population, so there were a fraction of the private homes with basements, garages, and attics that there would be in even a small town. In other words, the places where one could hide a victim or a car or a crime. And the three of us all had police experience and the authority—well, some authority—to demand and get answers and access if we really needed it.

On the other hand, most of my career had been spent looking for singular items and usually with a particular someone actively trying to hide them from me. The odds of finding something as ubiquitous as "a car" or "a person" were . . . well, let's just say if I still had my day job, I wouldn't feel like I had a chance unless I had a warrant, ten more cops to go door to door along the strip, and an Amber Alert notifying every driver on the interstate.

And we didn't have any of that.

Chuck kept the Integra crawling along at twenty or so to give us a chance to look over each parking lot and storefront on our side. Once or twice, cars ran up on us and hung on our bumper until Chuck irritably waved them around. A guy in a silver SUV pulled around and matched our speed so that the passenger could start screaming the riot act through her window, but she shut her trap and they scampered away when Chuck pulled out his badge and slapped it, face out, against the glass.

Several of the lots were empty and we gave them no more than a cursory glance. Two had drive-thrus or wide delivery alleys that required investigation, but we found nothing but Dumpsters and chain-link fencing in back. All were well lit and deserted—no Mustang, no Lucy, no exchange. After fifteen minutes, we'd covered half of our assigned end of the strip and I wasn't feeling good about our chances.

"Chuck, even if they label Lucy a runaway, I think it's time to call in the cavalry—" I began.

"Wait," he interrupted, pointing. "What's that?"

We were pulling adjacent to a restaurant, a retro-styled diner with polished aluminum sides like an old Airstream trailer. Inside, yellow lights revealed sleepy-looking waitresses shuffling between tables with coffeepots and menus. Most of the patrons huddled in booths, although a few sat at the counter in a scene reminiscent of *Nighthawks*—sans the moody romanticism and the classy dress. The thought of the coffee being poured inside made my stomach gurgle and my heart ache, but what had caught Chuck's attention were seven cars hunkered down in the lot. All but one of them were bunched around the door. Not surprising, considering the weather. The odd car out, however, was a black Mustang GT, parked in the farthest corner of the lot, at least five spaces away from its nearest neighbor. Compared to the others, it had only a light dusting of snow on its trunk and roof, and the tracks leading from the entrance to its stall were still visible. It hadn't been there long.

"That's it," Chuck said, his voice strung tight as a wire. "You ready?"

"Just drag him out of the car?" I asked. "Assuming they're in there?"

"He might be packing," Chuck said, understanding my question, "but he's not expecting us. He thinks he's meeting his payday. And there's no reason to keep his gun trained on Lucy. She's not going anywhere at this stage and he wouldn't shoot her even if she was."

Good enough for me. "Let's do it. I got passenger's side."

Chuck wheeled into the parking lot and pulled in behind the Mustang, blocking it in. We jumped out and raced to either side of the muscle car. Adrenaline was racing through my arms and legs, making them feel itchy, but I ignored the sensation and drew my gun. In two steps, I was next to the car, close enough to hear a bumping sound coming from inside.

I ripped open the passenger's door with my left hand, keeping my gun trained on the space behind the window while Chuck did the same on the other side. Hot, moist air spilled out of the car. I caught a flash of legs, revealing a length of upper thigh, the skin stark white in the darkness of the car's interior. A girl screamed at my intrusion and tried to climb into the backseat. A small part of my brain noticed that she wore—rather incongruously, I thought—fuzzy, shin-high fur boots, a short dress, and a leather jacket. Inside the diner, a few people glanced up from their cups.

"*Out of the car, motherfucker*," Chuck bellowed on his side, reaching in and grabbing a handful of hair. He dragged a man out of the car and shoved him face-first into the snow.

With more finesse and care, I leaned in and got hold of the arm of the girl in the passenger's seat, tugging her out into the light. "Lucy?" I asked. The girl's black hair cascaded forward, hiding her face, and I bent down to look under the curtain.

"Who the hell is Lucy?" she said, ripping my hand away. She ran a hand through her hair, revealing her comely—but very Caucasian and definitely *not* sixteen-year-old—face. Her lipstick was smeared and blue eyes glared back at me. I blinked. Not the reception I'd been expecting.

Chuck was screaming obscenities at the driver on the other side of the car and wasn't exactly beating him—yet—electing, instead, to lift him by the collar of his coat and slam him onto the ground like he was a pile of laundry. He raised his gun and pointed it at the back of the guy's head. The look on my friend's face was not good.

"Chuck!" I yelled, skidding and sliding as I came around the back of the car. I grabbed at his arm. "Chuck!"

Chuck tried to pull away and, for one dizzying moment, the barrel of his gun was pointed at my face. I ducked and used both of my hands to point his hand skyward. A weird noise was coming out of his throat.

"It's not him," I shouted. "It's not Lucy. *Chuck!* Listen to me!"

Something I said got through. Chuck stopped body-slamming the driver long enough for the guy to roll over and backpedal away, the heels of his shoes slipping in the snow, his eyes wide and as round as eggs. We didn't have a description of the guy we were looking for, but my intuition told me that the fiftyish white guy with an expression of stark terror on his face was not the hardened, lifelong criminal we were looking for.

"Jesus Christ," the guy whimpered. "Please . . ."

Chuck stared down at him, his face stricken. Snow continued to fall, fat flakes that stuck to our hair and coats, not melting. Quicker on the uptake than her man, the girl sensed we'd made a colossal mistake and began yelling, then threatening lawsuits and damages. I reached forward and helped the man to his feet. Without a word, Chuck went back to his car and got in.

"What was *that* about?" the man asked. "Did my wife send you?"

"Mistaken identity," I said. "Big time. Sorry about that."

"Sorry?" the girl said, overhearing me as she came around the car. She stuck a finger in my face. "You shove a damn *gun* in our faces and you think sorry is going to cover it?"

I gave her a look, then turned to the man. "You want to report this to the police? First thing they'll do is call your house to confirm your identity. Second thing they'll do is tell whoever answers where you are. And who you were with."

"Let's . . . let this one go, Maggie," the man said, his eyes sliding from mine. He brushed the last of the snow from his jeans and got back into the Mustang. The girl looked furious, but she could either follow his example or stand in the snow and argue with me. She settled for giving me the finger and jumping into the passenger's side.

"Carry on," I said. "If you can."

I got back in the Integra. The car was moving before I was completely inside. Chuck pulled out of the lot, took a right, and we continued the search.

After a minute, I said, "Was it close?"

"It was close," he said.

"Want to talk?"

"No."

I nodded and looked out the window.

CHAPTER THIRTY-FOUR

Sarah had to shake herself every few minutes. Not because she was tired, though she was, but because she was looking at the same homogeneous signs and storefronts offered in every highway rest stop in five states. The pizza joint was followed by a sub shop, which bordered a gas station that shared a driveway with a waffle house, which was adjacent to another gas station. Two years as a TFC and she'd already seen so many versions of the same roadside lineup that she was having trouble even remembering where she was. Familiarity really did breed contempt. Or, in this case, blindness.

But that wasn't how you spotted one black Mustang among the dozens of cars already plying the roads. You weren't going to pick out a frantic face pressed against the window if you were zoning out.

So she forced herself to choose a significant detail from each building. The tire center had six windows, the convenience store had five. The waffle shop by the exit had a second floor—was it fake or did they have a use for it? That motel had so many lights on that you could probably see it from space but that one . . .

. . . *that* one was dark as sin. Sarah sat upright. She actually *had* zoned out there for a second, but her wandering eyes had stopped cold on the dim silhouette of a building on a slight rise overlooking the strip. It was on one of the spurs she'd spotted on the map. It was completely dark, not just closed for the night. She'd already seen three or four daytime-only businesses and there was always at least a bright spotlight above the entrance or a glow coming from an inside lamp.

Sarah caught the right to get to the spur, turning the wheel hand over hand, considering her decision. Not ten minutes ago, the three of them had decided that Eddie would choose a clean, well-lighted place for the exchange, with just enough traffic to blend in. The deserted shell of the . . . Calloway Motel, the sign said as the road wound up the hill, was precisely the kind of place Eddie would not pick, according to their theories.

But it still made sense to check it out, she told herself. It was going to have a great view of the road below. If it was truly deserted, then there was literally no one to interrupt the trade. And it was still only a minute from the exit to the turnpike and the highway. Maybe it was more likely that they'd pick a restaurant parking lot, but it wasn't impossible that they'd choose an abandoned motel, either. Dropping her speed to a crawl, she crested the small butte and eased into the motel parking lot.

She wrinkled her nose as her headlights swept over the front of the building. Time had not been kind to the Calloway. The ramshackle motel looked as glum and down in the mouth as anything she'd ever seen in Baltimore. Architecturally, the building had been built in a Swiss chalet style, with a high, peaked roof reminiscent of Alpine villages, but the effect was ruined by the modern attic vents at the top of the gable—and the bent and twisted louvers of the vents meant the Calloway wasn't truly vacant; it was now home to a family of raccoons. That was something a childhood spent in rural Maryland told her was for sure. Gutters sagged and had fallen to the ground in many places. The windows that weren't boarded up were broken. Someone had made a small effort at renovation—there was an industrial-sized Dumpster in the back, evidence of some renovation, maybe. But it wasn't nearly enough to rescue the place.

So far, however, none of that would keep it from being a great meeting place for two crooks, though there was no evidence of it now. She completed her circuit of the place, then pulled close to the farthest edge of the lot, nearly dangling the front bumper over the lip of the hill to get a view of the strip. The perspective wasn't quite good enough to give her a clean look, however, so she sighed, zipped up her parka, then reached into the glove compartment for a pair of binoculars. She put her hands over the heating vents for courage, then stepped out of the cruiser and walked to the edge of the lot to scan the businesses below.

It was like a bad version of Monopoly. The storefronts below were laid out in two simple grids on either side of the main drag. Each mercantile enterprise was lined cheek by jowl next to its neighbor, trying its best to hook the schools of fish that swam by day and night on their way to the main flow of the highway. Sweeping the binoculars side to side, she checked each lot and storefront in turn, seeing little of note.

Sarah lowered the glasses, chewing her lip. She was getting lost in the details—the opposite of her previous problem of being *too* close to the minutiae as she drove by the storefronts. What was the big picture?

Her eyes were drawn to a bright bank of floodlights at the far end of the strip. The On Ramp, the largest business in Breezewood by far, dwarfed even the dozen-pump gas stations with car wash and convenience store. It was the one that stood out, the one that didn't share parity with its neighbors to the east and west. She raised the glasses again and panned them over the lot.

She'd been through Breezewood a dozen times and had known about the On Ramp—you couldn't drive through the town and not see it—but she'd never paid much attention to the fact that it was at least as large in the back as the front. Obviously catering to truckers, there were long parking bays and diesel pumps for convenience, and no doubt a back door to the main building just for the long-haulers. There were trucks there now, in fact, their owners probably asleep in the cabs before hitting the road.

Visibility wasn't great—the back of the On Ramp was not near the main road and the trailers were so high that, even from her vantage point on the hill, they hid whatever was right beside them. Although most of the other rigs were dark, the headlights of one were on, the driver having turned the cold engine over earlier, getting ready to start the day. After a moment, the truck eased forward like a dinosaur waking from sleep, lumbering toward the road. The rig rounded the front of the On Ramp and passed the parked cars of the tourists and commuters. With little traffic on the road, it turned onto the main drag without pausing and headed toward the turnpike at speed.

A chill went through her. It had taken the truck thirty seconds from the time it had started moving to the point where it had passed out of sight. If she knew Breezewood, and wanted to pull off an exchange like Eddie was attempting, you could hardly ask for a better location.

It was the On Ramp. It had to be.

She fumbled for her phone with gloved hands that couldn't dial a number. Shaking her glove off, she raised a finger to start dialing when, from behind her, a car horn honked, a long, brassy wail that made her jump.

She started to turn . . . then froze before she was halfway around. Cold, hard steel pressed against the back of her head, just above her last vertebra. It was the size and radius of a nickel, she thought distantly.

"Please don't do that, Officer," a voice said from behind her.

CHAPTER THIRTY-FIVE

Eddie stiffened, then leaned forward to peer out the windshield. Lucy glanced at him, then straightened in her seat to look, too—whatever was bad for Eddie was probably good for her.

Her heart jumped into her throat. Below them, a police cruiser crawled along the main road, pausing for a moment in front of each storefront. It turned into a few of the lots, but never completely stopped, describing a slow, serpentine path as it moved along, dipped in, then back out again. As they watched, it became apparent that the cruiser was taking more time in lots with cars in them and passing on those that were empty.

It was looking for something.

Eddie swore and turned the heat to its lowest setting, then dialed down the brightness of the dashboard lights. He slowly wrapped his hand around the gearshift, watching and waiting. On the road below, the cruiser stopped short of the spur road that led to the Calloway, as though the car itself was considering its options. Then, moving slowly, the cruiser made the right-hand turn that would bring it straight to the motel, its headlights illuminating broad curtains of falling snow.

With a dull chunking sound, Eddie eased the Mustang into reverse, then threw his arm over Lucy's seat and backed the car up slowly, keeping the normal roar of the engine to a low growl. The car caught and jerked as it slipped on the snow, but Eddie didn't ease off on the gas until he was behind the Calloway. Snow fell so fast their tracks were obliterated even as she watched. With easy skill, Eddie maneuvered the Mustang behind the bulk of the construction Dumpster, and shut off the car.

For a night that had been filled with virtually constant noise, the silence was sudden and oppressive. Only the smallest of sounds came to her. The engine ticked as it cooled. The snow made a slight patter as it hit the windshield and the roof. The distant thrum of the turnpike, previously inaudible over the noise of the engine, was like the hum of a dryer running in the basement or the buzz of her grandparents' old television set.

A sharp *click-clack* interrupted the silence as Eddie checked the action on his gun, then rested it in his lap. His face was expectant and tense. Their visibility from behind the Dumpster was limited to the wooded hillside behind the motel, but after a moment—as the police cruiser's headlights swept across the plateau—Lucy realized Eddie didn't need a perfect view. He only needed to see whether the car stopped or not.

The headlights lit the side of the motel as the cruiser pulled into the parking lot, then inched their way along as the cruiser made the wide turn to pull around the back of the building. Wild shadows danced against the hillside as the bright white light played over their hiding place. The cruiser was so close, she could hear the crunch of its tires on snow. Eddie's seat squeaked as he shifted in his seat. He swallowed audibly.

Her eyes dropped to look down at the gun in Eddie's hand, her body tingling. She could unlock the door, jump out, and start running. Scream loud enough and the cop would hear her, stop, and the nightmare would be over. A rescue was less than fifty feet away, less than thirty seconds away. If she dared.

But the gun was just sitting in his lap and he was obviously ready to use it. A muscle in the back of his hand was fluttering, like there was a bird trapped underneath the skin. If she tried to run, how fast could he raise his arm, aim, and pull the trigger? In no time at all. She would barely have her hand on the door handle before he shot her. But when would she get another chance?

Her hand began to creep toward the button of the door lock. The cruiser's headlights were directly on the Dumpster now and she could feel Eddie tense beside her . . . then the headlights moved on as the car made the wide turn. Their angle from behind the Dumpster gave them a slice of visibility, however, and she could tell by the headlights that the cruiser had slowed, then stopped altogether as it approached the edge of the parking lot where Eddie had been watching the strip below a few minutes before.

Eddie slipped the gun into his jacket, went to turn on the ignition . . . then hesitated, thinking. Her hand was almost to the door handle when he leaned across her without warning and popped open the glove compartment. Inside was a roll of duct tape.

"Turn towards the door," he said, shoving her in the back to turn her around in the seat.

"What?" she said, but he'd already grabbed both of her arms, then pinned her hands together with just one of his. Using his teeth and remaining hand, he got the roll of tape going and wound it around her wrists ten or twelve times. He leaned over awkwardly and did the same for her legs just below the knees, then he pushed her back in the seat so that she was sitting against her hands. He ripped off a short piece of tape, which he slapped over her mouth.

He pulled his gun out and said, "Don't move."

She nodded. He opened his door to a cold blast of air, then shut it carefully. She watched as he went to the corner of the Dumpster, peered around it, then disappeared. Lucy sat for a minute, deciding what to do. She could kick off her tennis shoes to try and manipulate the lock and the door with her feet, but then she'd be hopping shoeless in two feet of snow. Maybe it was worth it, or maybe she would get ten feet away before Eddie caught her.

Wriggling her body, she pushed herself over the center console, despite the emergency brake jabbing her painfully in the ribs, then sideways onto the driver's side of the car. The extra angle was just enough to allow her to see past the corner of the Dumpster.

The police officer was standing on the edge of the parking lot overlooking Breezewood. Both of his—her?—hands were raised. Holding binoculars, maybe. Closer to Lucy, though, Eddie had used the cover of the motel to get closer to the cruiser and was now hunkered down near the back bumper of the car. As Lucy watched, Eddie came out from around the back of the cruiser, cradling the gun with both hands. He was five feet away when Lucy leaned forward and jammed her shoulder onto the car horn, shattering the soft silence of the night.

The police officer jumped at the sound, then started to turn. But Eddie had moved with surprising speed and had the barrel of his gun pressed to the back of the cop's head before she—Lucy could see it was a woman now—could fully turn around. In a matter of seconds, he had her handcuffs out as well as her gun and keys. As Lucy watched, Eddie cuffed the officer with her hands behind her back and then marched her backward to the rear of the cruiser. He opened the trunk using the cop's own keys, shoved her inside, then closed the lid. Eddie went back to the front and leaned into the driver's side. A moment later, the headlights disappeared and then the car was also turned off, giving off one last forlorn cloud of exhaust before it stopped.

Lucy, trembling, pressed herself into the passenger's seat as Eddie trotted back to the car. He opened the door and hopped in, giving her a look that turned her blood cold.

"Nice try," he said. "A little late, but nice try. Not too smart, though. If the cop had seen me, then I'd have to kill you both. But now we're all safe and that was the last chance you had for someone to find you. Might as well sit back and relax now."

Lucy sank back into the seat, a tear falling down her cheek as Eddie started the Mustang and pulled out of the motel parking lot.

CHAPTER THIRTY-SIX

Breezewood was as plebeian as Torbett remembered it, an accidental town created for no other reason than to satisfy the hunger of the traffic from two large roads that happened to intersect. Granted, that's how some of the world's greatest cities got their start, but no one was going to mistake Breezewood, Pennsylvania, for Paris, London, or Rome. As the town's own name implied, it was a place for people to sweep through, not stop and look. It was a delay on the way to somewhere else.

And that's all it means to me, he thought. A quick meeting, a mistake-free handoff, and then back on the road. His own "somewhere else," of course, was right back where he'd started, but richer by the company of one beautiful, virginal Korean girl.

He reviewed the precautions he'd already taken and the step-by-step moves he would have to make soon to mitigate any identification of himself, his car, or what he was about to do. Using major highways to get here had been nerve-racking and dangerous but necessary, given the short time frame for the exchange. His other precautions—no stops there or back to trace receipts, tinted windows to foil any odd identification by fellow travelers while on the road, and meticulous attention to every driving regulation to avoid being pulled over by the police—would have to do. As maddening as it was, he'd driven with the utmost circumspection, obeying every speed limit and using his turn signal like he was on his way to take his driver's test. And, while he was sure his Lexus had been photographed somewhere along the line since there was almost no way to avoid it these days, he'd paid cash at all tolls instead of the more convenient, but easily traceable, E-ZPass.

Eddie would also be getting cash, naturally, in nonsequential bills he'd gathered on various trips from around the country. Even the money bag was a nondescript, national brand of garbage bag that could be found in every grocery, department, and home goods store in North America. He'd worn gloves since the moment he'd started the car and they'd stayed on throughout. They would be destroyed along with #5 as soon as he returned home. As long as Eddie was right about the back of the On Ramp being camera-free and close to the highway, he'd be safely in and out of the sorry little town of Breezewood in less than fifteen minutes.

And back home, with his newest toy, by brunch.

◆ ◆ ◆

"Nothing. There's nothing here," Chuck said, his voice rising.

We'd made our way down Breezewood's main drag, checked every parking lot, back alley, and spur road . . . and come up empty. Even counting our bust of the Unfaithful Husband and his paramour, the entire search had taken just twenty-three minutes. The town simply wasn't that big and, with Sarah's help, we'd only had to cover half of it.

The alternatives weren't encouraging. They might've already been here earlier, so we might've missed the handoff. They might be in Sarah's territory, but she hadn't found them yet or she'd also missed them.

Or, worst of all, the entire guess was wrong and they weren't even in Breezewood, maybe not even in the state. We were going on a tip from a hooker who had only a passing interest in seeing us bust her pimp . . . and that was it. We had nothing else.

"Let's start back and check the lots again," I said. "I'll touch base with Sarah, see if she's found anything."

"She would've called," Chuck said. I agreed with him, but we both knew that doing something constructive was better than sitting there.

I pulled out my phone and dialed her number. It rang three, four, five times, then went to voice mail. I frowned and punched redial. Nobody would ignore a call in this situation, especially, I got the feeling, someone as responsible and motivated as Trooper First Class Haynesworth. Five rings and voice mail again.

"No answer," I said, my mind going over the possibilities.

Chuck glanced over. "Straight to voice mail or did it ring?"

"It rang five times. She's not answering."

He shook his head slightly. "What's she doing?"

I got a sick, twisty feeling. She was the rookie, I was the thirty-year pro, and Chuck was more than competent enough to handle his end of things. I should've gone with her. "Forget this end of town, head towards her half."

Chuck punched the gas, shifted the Integra to third, and we tore up the road.

◆ ◆ ◆

Despite all her training, despite hours in the classroom warning her about the potential for being in something much like this situation, Sarah's first reaction was panic.

When she'd felt the cold steel of the gun barrel against the back of her head, she was sure he was going to kill her. Even when he'd locked her in the trunk instead of shooting her on the spot, it didn't erase the fear—he might set the car on fire or put it in neutral and push it over the lip of the hill. She'd had to grit her teeth to keep from screaming.

But in the distance she heard the deep gurgle of a powerful engine start—the Mustang, surely—and for some reason that popped the balloon of fear. It didn't follow that Eddie was going to torch the cruiser if he was leaving so quickly. Or, why would he go back and start the Mustang if he was going to send the cruiser careening over the hill? Which is when her brain finally kicked in and cleared the air.

He was here to make a sale, not kill people.

Eddie had only one goal: to meet the person who was buying Lucy. To do that, he needed to be on time and he especially needed to keep from attracting attention. Turning a state police cruiser into a bonfire on top of a hill was not the way to stay inconspicuous. Pushing it over a hill to crash into the back of a diner was going to attract attention. He didn't want to kill her; he just wanted her out of the way long enough to get his money.

Armed with that thought, she put her mind and priorities in order. *Get your head on straight, girl. Think about what you need to do.* First, she needed to get her hands free. Second, she needed to warn Rhee and Singer. Third, she needed to get out of the car. Number four was more of a want than a need: she *wanted* to kick Eddie's ass so far up around his ears he'd have to take his pants down to hear right.

Freeing her hands wasn't easy, but not impossible. Eddie was an amateur and had been in a hurry, that much was clear. With more experience or another minute to think about it, he would've twisted the bracelets on the cuffs to clamp them close to her wrists—and he hadn't. She'd had the presence of mind to not demonstrate just how much slack she had when he'd frog-marched her back to the cruiser's trunk.

Nor had he searched her pockets for anything but the car keys and her gun. He hadn't taken her phone or, maybe more importantly, her spare set of handcuff keys. Unfortunately, those were in a front pocket. Moving with care so that she didn't tighten the cuffs herself, she eased onto her side and began stretching her arms out and around her body, using her belt loops as tiny handholds for her fingers to inch along her waist.

Midway through the effort, her phone rang in her pocket—Singer or Rhee, it had to be. They would have to wait until she got a hand free. Moving with exquisite care, she pushed and pulled, gasping as the ligaments in her shoulders and elbows were tested to the breaking point. She took one last, deep breath, let it out, then lurched forward. Her fingers caught on the edge of the front pocket and she strained her fingers as far as she could, using all of the slack he'd given her to dive into the pocket. One agonizing moment later, her fingers tickled the round piece of steel that was the key ring and gently pulled it out of her pocket.

Despite the cold, she was sweating. She paused for a moment, collecting herself, then took a deep breath and began manipulating the little keys until the cuffs came free with a familiar snap. She breathed out a huge breath and massaged her wrists long enough to get the feeling back, then dug out her phone and hit the call-back button to tell Singer that, if they didn't move now, it was going to be too late.

◆ ◆ ◆

The rest stop was right where Eddie had said it would be, looking just like he'd said it would look, brightly lit and modern, with enough cars to give them the kind of bustling cover they needed to pull off the exchange. It was a relief, actually. The motel where they'd met last time was practically deserted—it was a wonder that the local cops didn't simply sit in its parking lot and arrest the drug dealers and junkies as they arrived, a kind of criminal drive-thru.

And it was close to the turnpike on-ramp, too. He stifled a titter. Hence the name. *On Ramp*. Trust the local yokels to pick the most obvious moniker for their businesses. Whatever they called it, it looked to be the perfect place for the exchange. It was going to take him all of five minutes to conclude their business. With, he hoped, zero interference from the few bleary-eyed tourists and truckers at the place.

For the first time since he'd cemented the initial agreement with Eddie, Torbett was feeling relaxed and confident that the deal would go through. He was taciturn and skeptical to begin with, and this arrangement had seemed particularly cursed from the outset. The number of calls and points of contact they'd had to make throughout the night still made him anxious. But, he had to admit, while an obstacle-free exchange was always preferable, wasn't there something even more satisfying in overcoming challenges to reach the same point?

Torbett signaled conscientiously and made the slow, smooth turn into the On Ramp's front parking lot. Eddie had said to ignore the lot and head for the back, where the truckers parked their "rigs."

Yes, there was the driveway—an extension of the parking lot, really, it was so wide—clearly signed for trucks. Torbett followed it around back, looking for cameras on the building's corners or roof, but either they had none or he couldn't see them at this angle. The lot was well lit and had maybe twenty triple-length stalls marked off with white paint. Six semitrucks sat like slumbering giants, unmoving and inert. Four were bunched together, while the two others were off at opposite ends of the lot, perhaps looking for some privacy or quiet.

Torbett pulled near the far end of the bunch of four, attempting to shield his car from the On Ramp's main building, but not so close that the trucker next to him got curious. Then he turned off his lights and began to wait.

It was the last thing he wanted to do. Now that he was so close, the anticipation ran through him like a tiny electric current. A muscle in his cheek ticked and he had an erection that strained against his trousers. He did some deep-breathing exercises in an effort to calm himself, but it only got his circulation pumping, sending more oxygen to his already-hyperactive muscles.

To pass the time, he reached under the seat and pulled out a black zippered case the size of a shaving kit. Inside was a small glass vial and two syringes—low-dose Nembutal in case his gift showed some reluctance in adjusting to her new role on the way home. Two syringes in case the lesson had to be repeated.

A noise to his left made him drop the case to the floor in a panic. A moment later, the passenger's-side door to the truck next to him opened. Despite the tinted windows, he sank down in his seat as one slim bare leg, then another, swung out the side of the cab. A willowy girl in a miniskirt and patched denim jacket grabbed the chrome help-me-up next to the door, then swung out of the cab. She hopped down to the ground and slammed the door shut, tucking something inside a pocket of the jacket as she did so.

She started in surprise at the sight of the Lexus, seemed to consider something, then began a slow walk to Torbett's side of the car. He knew the tinting kept her from seeing inside, but he got the feeling that she was staring directly at him anyway. She wasn't really his type—too tall, too thin—but she had wide blue eyes with a girlish spray of freckles over the pale white skin of her nose and cheeks. Her hair was long and black—probably not natural, but the contrast of it against the swirling white snow had him entranced. His erection swelled painfully and he adjusted himself as she sauntered to the driver's-side window and drummed her fingernails lightly against the glass.

He rolled the window down halfway. "Yes?"

She ducked her head and looked in with a smile. "Hi there."

"Hi." He swallowed.

"I never seen a car like this before." She was nineteen, maybe, and at this distance he could see the skin wasn't flawless. Acne and too much makeup took some of the shine away. There was a bruise high on one cheek and the eyes were tired. But she had a cant to her head and a quirk to her mouth that had him squeezing the steering wheel.

"I imagine not," he said. *Dare I eat this peach?* It would be so stupid, so against the rules. But he'd been breaking rules all night and it hadn't mattered. And if one was good, wouldn't two be better? It was Fate, dropping a pair of nubile girls into his lap in payment for all the hurdles she'd strewn in front of him before. And rules were meant to be broken.

The girl saw something in his eyes and her smile became knowing. She raised an eyebrow.

"Would you like to see how it handles?" he asked.

"I sure would," she said, moving around the front of the car.

In the time it took her to get to the passenger's side, he had the first syringe ready and waiting.

◆ ◆ ◆

The home stretch. The home stretch. The home stretch.

It was all Eddie could think about as he made the turn off the spur from the Calloway and onto the main road. The On Ramp was less than a quarter mile away and surely Torbett was there by now. Having to take care of the cop had put him behind, but with luck the delay had been only enough to get Torbett to Breezewood and not so much that the guy panicked and ran.

Light crept over the hills surrounding the town, although the valley was still dark. It was late enough that cars and trucks were starting to fill the roads, their headlights pushing back both the receding night and the snow that continued to fall in waves. The extra traffic slowed him down at several of the lights, which gave him time to think.

Specifically, it gave him time to worry about what the cop had been doing at the Calloway. He'd had enough presence of mind to recognize the cruiser as a Maryland state trooper's. Not that weird for Breezewood, probably, since the town wasn't far from the border. But the cop had seemed to be looking for something specific. Did every trooper get out of their car and scan the countryside with binoculars at five in the morning? And, maybe it was his imagination, but she'd done a double take just as she'd panned across the On Ramp.

"Shit," he said out loud, making Lucy flinch. They must've found Gerry's body or uncovered something about Lucy's kidnapping. Maybe Tuck or one of his asshole roomies had blabbed and someone had thought to call the cops. But how'd they manage to trace him to Breezewood in only a few hours?

It didn't matter. He had to go through with the buy. And maybe he wasn't in as much trouble as he feared. The cop had been *searching*, not *watching*. That meant that they knew a lot, but not everything. They might be looking for him, but they didn't know about the meet, or if they did, they were still looking for it. If Torbett was there with the money, they could make the exchange and go their separate ways before anyone found the cop, figured out the meet was at the On Ramp, or stopped them.

But it was going to be close. He might have only a matter of minutes before the law descended on the place. And sitting in traffic wasn't where he wanted to be when that happened. With a quick glance in the mirror, Eddie wheeled around the cars in front of him and into the oncoming turning lane, then floored it. Honking the horn, he shot through the intersection, narrowly missing a flatbed truck making the turn onto I-70, and flew up the slight rise to the On Ramp. He whipped the Mustang across the road and On Ramp's tourist lot, then slowed down to take the driveway back to the truckers' lot.

Eddie leaned forward, scanning the large asphalt plain. The lot had been plowed for the truckers' convenience, but there were only a handful of rigs actually parked. A few diesel pumps sat gathering snow on one side of the lot, empty and waiting for customers. No cops so far, at least none out in the open, which meant they weren't here, since this wouldn't be an undercover sting. If they'd been on to him, the parking lot would've been lousy with law enforcement, their lights flashing from

Breezewood to Baltimore. Still, Eddie made a slow, cautious circuit, finally coming to the far side of a gathering of three or four rigs.

There. Torbett's Lexus parked cheek by jowl next to a semi, as though trying to hide. Figures—he should've guessed the most paranoid man he'd ever met would park in as inconspicuous a spot as possible.

Eddie frowned. There was something wrong. The passenger's door wasn't fully closed and the car was rocking back and forth. He pulled the Mustang close to the Lexus and hopped out.

A girl with a miniskirt was sitting half in the passenger's seat with one foot on the ground. She was struggling with Torbett, who was behind the wheel like he was supposed to be, but he had one hand wrapped in the girl's hair while the other held a . . . needle? The girl was holding the syringe away with both hands but losing the battle. Torbett's face rippled with emotions—anger, fear, excitement. He seemed to relish the girl's resistance.

"What the fuck are you doing?" Eddie yelled.

Torbett raised his head, bewildered. He blinked a few times, as if Eddie's words had snapped him out of a daze. Eddie reached in, grabbed the girl by the arm and pulled her out, then shoved her toward the main building. She took a few steps away, sobbing, then stopped and started screaming half-formed words at them.

"What is *wrong* with you?" Eddie said, ignoring her. "We don't have time for this shit."

"I . . . I wanted another one," Torbett said, with the face and guile of a five-year-old. "She was right there."

"Jesus Christ. What do you need with a truck-stop whore? I've got what you asked for, right here. Remember? Lucy? The girl you've been dreaming about?"

Torbett nodded and blinked, nodded and blinked.

"Okay," Eddie said, not convinced Torbett was completely there. "You got the money?"

"Yes. In the backseat."

"All right. Let's do this, then. The girl for the money."

Torbett's eyes slid past him. "You mean that girl?"

Eddie spun around. Hobbled by the duct tape wound around her knees and wrists, Lucy was stumbling awkwardly away from the cars and toward the On Ramp's outbuildings at the back of the lot. It wouldn't lead her anywhere—the entire place was surrounded by a chain-link fence—but she didn't know that.

"God*damn* it," Eddie swore and took off after her. Lucy was almost to the truckers' lounge and he was halfway across the lot when, with a roar, a silver Integra with a raised spoiler and gleaming rims shot through the driveway and flew into the lot.

◆ ◆ ◆

I wasn't sure what to expect as we rocketed into the On Ramp's back forty. We'd spent the past eight hours in the dark, not even knowing if we were in the right *state*. Only Sarah's breathless phone call gave us any kind of confirmation that we'd been right all along, but even she was playing a hunch when she told us to head for the rest stop by the turnpike entrance, that that's where the trade had to be going down.

So it was with fingers crossed but still some doubts that we hit the truckers' area of the On Ramp at seventy miles an hour. Chuck slammed on the brakes and we skidded to a stop, the ice and snow carrying us to within a few scary feet of a row of diesel pumps. I sat forward, scanning the lot, taking in the environment, trying to pull out details. But the scene was crazy enough that we just *had* to be in the right place.

A pack of trucks was bunched in the middle of the lot. Two had lights on in the cabs and the truckers inside were illuminated like figurines in a shadow box, frowning and looking out their side windows. A deep blue or black Lexus was parked near the far truck, with a black Mustang sitting next to it. The Lexus's driver's-side door was open and a tall, chubby man with a comb-over and no winter coat was standing in the crotch of the door and the car, looking toward me and Chuck with a bland expression. He hadn't started by looking in our direction, though—he'd swung his head around from watching . . .

"Lucy!" Chuck yelled and jumped out of the Integra.

A slim figure was at the far end of the lot, running—or trying to run—in strange, herky-jerky strides toward a small outbuilding that said "SHOWERS." I squinted and realized her arms were behind her back.

Chasing her was a tall man—Eddie, it had to be him—in a black jacket. He should've caught up with her, but he was slipping on the icy asphalt and hadn't made it even halfway across the lot. Chuck split the difference between them and started running, screaming, "Freeze!"

I popped my door open, jumped out, and started for the Lexus. Chuck's challenge had reached Eddie and he stopped and turned smoothly in our direction, almost as if he'd been expecting us. A hand dipped inside his coat and pulled out something black and blocky.

"*Gun!*" I yelled as I threw myself flat. Peripherally, I was aware that Chuck had seen it, too, but he was closer and more exposed, having tried to cross the no-man's-land of the middle of the lot.

The most vulnerable of all of us, though, was Lucy.

Things slowed down and crystallized like the ice around us, and I watched as Eddie turned and—instead of taking the shot at Chuck or me—trained his sights on Lucy as she hobbled toward the edge of the lot. I raised my head from the mound of snow, feeling a terrible, metallic weight drop through me. If he was going to shoot her, I would be too late. I scrambled to get to one knee so I could try a futile shot to stop him or at least get his attention. Someone screamed a name, a word, an animal sound.

For a split second, Lucy's life hung in the air, ready to be plucked. But a strange grimace crossed Eddie's face and he swung his attention—and the gun—back in our direction. I threw myself flat again and, a moment later, a stunning, ratcheting sound filled the air, like the loudest firecracker you've ever heard, but evenly spaced and faster by a mile. A mix of fear and animal-level adrenaline washed over me. There's nothing quite like the sound of automatic gunfire to make your body tap into its deepest instincts and send you diving for cover. The bullets missed, plinking and pinging as they ricocheted off the tanks behind me. The heady stink of diesel gas filled the air a moment later.

I shoved my face into the snow, willing myself as flat as humanly possible. The burst stopped and I stumbled and clawed my way to the shelter of one of the big rigs. My hands burned from the snow and I banged my knee on the ice as I scrambled for safety. Another short burst of gunfire stitched the air, followed by four rapid claps, deeper in tone—Chuck returning fire. I poked my head out. The tall guy was still moving, but this time retreating toward his car, slipping another magazine into his gun as he ran. While his attention was turned toward Chuck, who was lying prone in the snow, I lined up on Eddie, pulled the trigger twice, and missed both shots. Chuck's gun spat again and Eddie screamed, or I imagined he did, and spun in place, but stayed on his feet and staggered toward his car.

I ducked as he fired another short burst, wild and without aim, then took a step away from the truck to get a clear shot. My feet were placed shoulder-width apart, both hands steady on the gun. I took a deep breath, aimed, and—

There was a small *pop* behind me, a sizzling sound, then an explosion took me off my feet like I'd been kicked in the pants by an NFL lineman. I landed face-first five or six feet away. Heat rolled over the lot in a wave, with an ugly cloud of fumes chasing it. A second, smaller explosion followed, carrying its own shock wave of heat and petroleum stink.

I was facedown on the ground, with my world tilted six degrees off level. Falling debris hit truck hoods and specked my hands. A lame attempt to stand was unsuccessful and a grotesque snow angel formed under me from the flailing of my arms and legs. Shattered glass mixed with the ice in front of my face, sparkling like pixie dust. My ears were ringing, and I felt rather than heard the purr of a powerful engine pass near me as the Lexus shot out of the lot.

A determined push got me to my hands and knees, then a supreme effort got me to a kneeling position. I wasn't injured, but bruised, physically exhausted, and probably slightly concussed. Not surprisingly, the combination had me feeling highly unmotivated and only the fact that Chuck and Lucy might be hurt got me up off the snow. I looked to my left. Two of the three diesel pumps had shot into the sky like flares, taking Chuck's precious Integra with them. The car that had carried us through the night looked like a smoking war relic from the battlefields of El Alamein or Iraq.

Using the truck fender to get to my feet, I staggered to the middle of the lot. A quick glance to the side showed no sign of Eddie. Chuck was shaking his head and kicking his legs like I'd been doing a moment ago. Where I'd been knocked down by the blast, though, it looked like he'd been conked by a flying piece of his own car. I checked him for the obvious stuff, but he slapped my hands away when I told him to lie still while I went for help.

"Lucy?" he croaked.

Against my better judgment, I helped him to his feet and we stumbled toward the outbuilding she'd been running to. We found her there, cowering in a corner where the bricks of the building met the chain-link fencing. She was covered in duct tape and snow, but cried out when she saw Chuck. The two of them became a mess of tears, cursing, and laughter as he tried to unwind the tape from her wrists and ankles and knees. When she was finally free, they hugged like they were trying to squeeze each other in two.

I wandered away to give them their moment. Truckers were coming out of their cabs, wary and wide-eyed, while a small crowd of fearless, apron-wearing kitchen staff from the On Ramp were gathered at the back entrance, looking at the fuel pumps like it was the aftermath of a Fourth of July.

Gun at the ready, I limped over to the black Mustang, which was stippled from the shrapnel. I shuffled around the front bumper, giving myself plenty of room to hit the ground again if I needed to.

I didn't. Eddie lay on his back, his face locked in a grin or a grimace. Blood seeped into the snow from several spots on his left side. His gun was lying in the snow ten feet away, but I didn't lower my gun in case it wasn't the only heat he'd been packing. It was a needless precaution. Even if he had another weapon, he wasn't in any shape to use it. His chest heaved in uneven motions and he keened in pain, continuous and low.

I knelt beside him and flipped open his jacket. At least two of Chuck's bullets had caught him. The amount of blood he was losing didn't look good. My gaze flicked to his face where curiously colorless blue eyes looked back into mine.

"You . . . know . . . any . . . poetry, man?" he asked, then he was still.

Sirens bleated in the distance. I was still staring at the face of Eddie when I heard feet crunching in the snow. I turned to see Sarah walking toward me.

"I missed it," she said, her face a mix of anger and disbelief. "All this damn work and I missed it."

"No," I said, and stood. "You made it. As in, made it happen. These guys were a minute from making the handoff and would've been on the road in five minutes if it hadn't been for you. Lucy would be gone."

She looked down at Eddie. "I let him lock me in my own car. With my own cuffs. If he'd had more time, he might've killed me."

I reached out and squeezed her arm. Maybe I didn't know her well enough for the gesture, but her voice was full of self-reproach and that needed to stop. From what I'd seen, she was too good of a cop for her to lose any self-esteem on this. "He might've done a lot of things. But he didn't. And he won't, thanks to me and Chuck. And you."

Her look was still unhappy as she stared down at Eddie, but eventually her face relaxed a fraction and I saw a tiny smile. Behind us there was more crunching of snow, more feet. We turned to see Chuck guide Lucy over to us, his arm around her protectively. I stepped forward to close the gap. Lucy had been through enough—she didn't need to see the ugliest part.

"Singer," Chuck said. "Is he . . . ?"

I nodded and Lucy made a funny kind of moaning sigh. Chuck squeezed her arm and she put her head on his shoulder.

"I'm so glad we got here in time, Lucy," Sarah said, her eyes bright. "No one should go through what you did."

"Thank you," Lucy whispered. "Thank you so much."

A few of the falling flakes got into my own eyes, making them water, and then I discovered that I was taking part in a group hug. Which is how we remained until a dozen local and state police careened into the parking lot, lights and sirens on full blast, spilling out of their cruisers and emergency vehicles, barking questions, all of them wanting to know just what the hell we'd done to their little Town of Motels.

CHAPTER THIRTY-SEVEN

The trailer had made a small concession to the holidays. Feeble white Christmas lights outlined the door, plastic holly and ivy garland decorated the tiny, scrap wood front porch, and a "Merry Xmas!" banner hung from inside one window.

There was a single light on inside. Sherrie—dishwater-blonde hair pulled back in a ponytail, hollow-eyed, worn down to the essence—stood in front of the window, arms crossed and staring intently at the cinder drive where it came up to the trailer. She was dressed in a pale blue sweatshirt and pants two sizes too big. She smoked Camel Lights and played with her lower lip while she watched the road. It's where she'd stood since night had become morning and dark became light.

The six-by-eight space that passed for a living room smelled of weed and cigarette smoke. On the coffee table a box of wine lay on its side, spilling white Zinfandel onto the carpet drop by drop. Lauren was sprawled on the built-in sofa, an arm thrown across her forehead. She'd come to keep Sherrie company through the night, but had ended up just drinking most of the wine and getting baked into unconsciousness.

Sherrie didn't mind. Lauren's chatter would've driven her crazy as the hours passed without a call. She would've talked nonstop about what she was going to do to the place after Sherrie was gone, hardly able to contain herself at the prospect of having a trailer of her own instead of having to share with her sister or shacking up with her boyfriend. Sherrie could tune it out most of the time—what would it matter, since she was going someplace better?—but sure as shit Lauren would've noticed when her ride hadn't arrived and Sherrie's bags sat there by the door.

A cry from the bedroom in the back interrupted her thoughts and she stubbed out the cigarette quickly, then hurried down the hallway. She came back with a small bundle in a pink blanket covered in a Babar the Elephant print, a hand-me-down from another young mother that had moved out of the trailer park last summer and hadn't had room in the car for everything.

Swaying from side to side and bouncing the bundle occasionally, she hummed tunelessly and made baby talk. A note of desperation threaded her voice. The baby usually began wailing at five and didn't stop until it had cried itself back to sleep. But this day, to her relief, the little thing decided to stay quiet, leaving her to watch out the window, and wait.

The dark turned to false dawn and then to a true white-sky winter morning, when you weren't sure if you were looking at the falling snow or a rising sun. But to Sherrie, the most important thing—as she felt a deep, tearing sense of depression—was that nobody and nothing came up the drive to stop in front of her trailer to take her and her baby away.

"I guess your daddy's not coming, after all," she whispered. A tear slipped down her cheek as she left the window and went to the tiny kitchen to fix the baby's formula. It would start crying if she didn't feed it soon.

CHAPTER THIRTY-EIGHT

The last of the electronics had been destroyed and the phones smashed. The Lexus was wiped down, inside and out, and he'd hired a service to take it away to be detailed for a third time as a precaution. He'd shredded, then burned, his albums, nearly crying as he did so. They were the things he valued the most about his calling, both as a prize for him to relish and the lasting tribute to all the work he'd put into pursuing, gathering, and cataloging. He'd often dreamed of some future archaeologist or antiques hunter finding them in the ruins of his home and the shocked titillation they would experience leafing through them.

Torbett paced down to his office, absorbed by his thoughts. All of it was gone now. Thanks to Eddie and his incompetence. If he'd only listened to his own instinct . . . His gut had been telling him to drop the deal and move on, but thoughts of the little Asian girl had clouded his thinking so thoroughly that—instead of acting with the consummate care and caution that had protected him for years—he'd risked everything.

One more glance around the office, he thought. Tired eyes missed important clues, but it made him feel better to be doing something, to give himself the illusion that he was being conscientious and vigilant. Drawers, card files, and cabinets were clean and held only personal finances and the like. Boring, pedestrian, utterly normal. He turned his attention to the new laptop he'd purchased just this week. His workaday files were in place, with no trace of anything untoward. The only item which law enforcement might look at even mildly askance was the program that ran his security cameras, but even that was common enough now that cops barely gave those kinds of things a second glance, especially for the city's wealthiest citizens.

To test the system, Torbett launched the program that patched his laptop into the split-screen video feeds of the cameras. Idly, he browsed the six panels that covered the entrances to his house, garage, and front gate.

Damn. Camera five was blacked out. It covered the glass doors of the veranda, the ones that led out to the garden. Zero visibility meant that the connection had come undone. Fixing it was a pain, and he was tempted to give himself a much-deserved break, but security wasn't something you waited on. Torbett retraced his steps back down the hall, through the dining room, and into the parlor which led out onto the veranda.

He considered getting a ladder and a few tools first—or at least a jacket for the cold—then, impatient, decided to simply eyeball the situation to see what had happened. He unlocked the glass doors and stepped outside, looking over and up to where the camera sat.

Then, suddenly, he was looking at a mound of snow three inches in front of his face. The right side of his face was freezing and, distantly, he realized he was lying prone, his body sprawled along the bricks of the veranda. The left side of his head throbbed with an acute pain that ran from his jaw, passed through his cheekbone, and on to his forehead. With a monumental effort, he rolled onto his side but had to stay that way, however, unable to raise himself to a sitting position. His arms were rubbery and useless. He wondered if he'd slipped on a patch of ice and concussed himself.

His eyesight was blurry and he raised a hand to check for blood. There was a little spot of the stuff, yes, but more alarming was a small noise to his right. He turned his head and his eyes widened, but he didn't have the mental acuity to do anything except stare at the two people, a man and a woman, standing on his veranda. They looked down at him with an expression of distaste, as though they were examining a stain and contemplating how to remove it.

Both were Asian, with black hair and the same slim, athletic build. The man was taller and had the kind of piercings and tattoos that, seen on the street or on the news, made Torbett curl his lip. The girl was slender, with a mane of black hair.

"You sure you want to do this?" the man asked, not taking his eyes off Torbett.

"If it's him," she replied.

"Sarah scooped his car's tags from the girl he tried to grab at the On Ramp, which is good enough for me," the man said. "Wouldn't fly with a grand jury, but that ain't our problem."

"Who," Torbett said, having trouble forming the word. His jaw was either broken or dislocated. "Who are you?"

The girl moved closer, then knelt in the snow. She was beautiful, Torbett thought. Her face could stop a man's heart and her eyes were a bottomless black well. As she bent her head near his, her hair swung down and brushed his face.

"I'm the package you ordered," she said, smiling for the first time. The expression was colder than the ice underneath his body and lacked any room for understanding or forgiveness. "And I'm here to deliver."

NOTES

I apologize for painting the town of Breezewood with an uncharitable brush. In my defense, the short strip connecting Interstate 70 with the Pennsylvania Turnpike isn't any better than I portray it here, but the land surrounding the intersection is quite beautiful, as is most of rural Pennsylvania and Maryland. If you find yourself in the area with an extra half hour, do yourself a favor and take a few lefts and rights off the beaten path.

The Calloway Motel is a fabrication, although there are one or two buildings in Breezewood that fit the description. The On Ramp is real, although the name has been changed. The activities that go on there are only my educated guess.

ACKNOWLEDGMENTS

I'd like to thank Detective Billy Woolf of the Fairfax County Police, who made the transition from the department's Gangs unit to become the single operational member of the Northern Virginia Human Trafficking Task Force. Detective Woolf was kind enough to sit down with me and guide me through some of the thornier and more misunderstood issues surrounding juvenile human trafficking from both the public perception and that of law enforcement. Thanks, Billy.

I learned a great deal about juvenile human trafficking through the Klaas Kids Foundation website (www.klaaskids.org) and what parents and citizens can do to help prevent childhood kidnappings and abuse. Visit Klaas Kids for resources, information, and help.

My editors Elyse Dinh-McCrillis and Michael Mandarano took a rough idea and helped make it into the book you have in your hands. Elyse and Michael, thank you.

Lastly, thank you to my editor, Kjersti Egerdahl, and the team at Thomas & Mercer for giving me the chance to show the world what Marty Singer is all about.

ABOUT THE AUTHOR

Photo © 2014 Sally Iden

Matthew Iden writes hard-boiled detective fiction, fantasy, science fiction, horror, thrillers, and contemporary literary fiction with a psychological twist. He is the author of the Marty Singer detective series:

A Reason to Live
Blueblood
One Right Thing
The Spike
The Wicked Flee

Visit www.matthew-iden.com for information on upcoming appearances, new releases, and to receive a free copy of *The Guardian: A Marty Singer Short Story*—not available anywhere else.

IF YOU LIKED *THE WICKED FLEE*...

Writers can only survive and flourish with the help of readers. If you like what you've read, please consider reviewing *The Wicked Flee* on Amazon.com or your favorite readers' website. Just three or four short sentences are all it takes to make a huge difference! Thank you.

STAY IN TOUCH

Please say hello via e-mail, matt.iden@matthew-iden.com, through Facebook at http://www.facebook.com/matthew.iden, or Twitter @CrimeRighter. I also enjoy connecting with readers and writers at my website, matthew-iden.com.